THESE HAUNTED HILLS

A COLLECTION OF SHORT STORIES

BOOK 3

Linda Hudson Hoagland (4)

Jan-Carol
Publishing, Inc

"every story needs a book"

These Haunted Hills
A Collection of Short Stories
Book 3
Published September 2021
Mountain Girl Press
Imprint of Jan-Carol Publishing, Inc
Copyright © 2021 Jan-Carol Publishing, Inc.

ISBN: 978-1-954978-22-5
Library of Congress Control Number: 2021947480

You may contact the publisher:
Jan-Carol Publishing, Inc.
PO Box 701
Johnson City, TN 37605
publisher@jancarolpublishing.com
www.jancarolpublishing.com

This is dedicated to all the talented authors for their participation in this collection of short stories, and to all the readers of Jan-Carol Publishing's books.

TABLE OF CONTENTS

An Appalachian Rainbow

Jan Howery

(Inspired by actual events)

"Jane! Time to come in," Paul hollered to her. "It's supper time!" Jane was a rambunctious, six year old little girl, and Paul had done his best in raising his daughter. Life had not been easy. When Jane was four years old, her mother, Beth, was killed in automobile accident. Beth was the bread winner of the family. After her death Paul found it difficult to pay all the bills. Paul worked part time as an early morning radio announcer and as a sales rep for the radio station selling radio advertising. He also sang in a local band, but when he received the first foreclosure notice on the house, he knew it was time to take action.

Paul sold the house before the bank took possession, and he was able to purchase a nice a mobile home. His parents had a small farm and their yard was almost an acre, so he moved it on his parents' property. His home fit perfectly in the back section of the yard, and being so close to his mom and dad meant dependable babysitters.

Also within walking distance was his granddad, Pappy. He would be there to help when his mom and dad were not available. Everyone was ecstatic and welcomed the opportunity to help with Jane, and she was excited to be closer to Nana, Papa, and Pappy.

But three months after they moved, Pappy, who adored Jane, passed away suddenly from a heart attack. He'd spent time with her, taken her on nature walks, and was always waiting for her when she got home from school. Jane loved Pappy, and while at first she seemed to accept his passing, in the last month or so Jane seemed to speak of Pappy more often.

"Jane! Come in now. And now means now!" Paul yelled out the door again.

Jane looked at her mud castle and thought, *I'll have to finish it tomorrow.* She ran through the front door and asked enthusiastically, "What's for supper?"

"Your favorite! Mac and cheese with a plain hot dog. But look at those hands! Go to your bathroom, take off your muddy coat and shoes, and wash your hands all the way up to the elbows. And do a good job," Paul instructed Jane.

Within a few minutes Jane returned to the kitchen and stuck out her hands for inspection.

"Jane, your hands are still pretty dirty," Paul said smiling. He walked Jane to her bathroom, which was a muddy mess, and helped her wash her hands and her face. They both returned to the kitchen. Paul grabbed the TV tables to set up in front of the chairs in the living room so they could watch TV as they ate. As he walked to the first chair Jane screamed, "No! Pappy's sitting there!"

Paul immediately turned and placed the table in front of the other living room chair. "No! Chief Running Rainbow's sitting there!"

"That's enough!" Paul snapped. "We'll sit where we need to be sitting anyway. At the kitchen table! And that's enough about Pappy and the Indian, Chief Running Rainbow, which by the way, you should refer to him as Native American."

"But, he's an Indian with feathers with rainbow colors in his hair. He's a Chief," Jane replied sternly.

"But I told you, Jane, Pappy is in Heaven with Momma, and the Indian is from your favorite book, *Broken Sky*. It isn't real," Paul said harshly.

Jane looked sad. "Pappy comes to see me. And Chief Running

Rainbow is my friend, and he comes to see me too!" Jane said defiantly.

Paul just ignored Jane's reply. "Eat your supper and we'll start on your homework," Paul instructed.

After supper, Paul cleaned the kitchen, helped Jane with her homework, bathed her, and got her into her PJ's for bed.

"Will you read to me from my Indian Chief book?" Jane asked as she crawled under the covers on her bed.

"No. It's bedtime. Here's your teddy bear and let's say your prayers, then it's time to go to sleep," Paul replied. Jane was asleep as soon as her little head hit her pillow.

The next morning, Paul was up early and dressed for work. He woke Jane and got her out of bed. "Jane, I'm going to take you to Nana's so she can get you dressed and ready for school."

Paul carried Jane to the back door of his Mom's house with a lunch that he had packed, and his mother met him at the door. "She's so sleepy," Nana said.

"Sorry, Mom, but I've got to get to the station early. We're working on trying to get things in place so that I can just work from home remotely. But as soon as it looks like it's going to work, we're offline," Paul frowned. "I packed a lunch and here's her clothes for the day."

"Oh my. I'll help some with that lunch," Nana said with a wink. "And her clothes are wrinkled. I'll take of that too."

"Thanks Mom." Paul gave his mother a hug.

* * *

The week moved quickly and soon enough it was Friday, the last day of school before the Thanksgiving holiday. Paul made arrangements for Jane to stay over the weekend with his mom and dad since the band was booked on Friday night, Saturday night, and on mid Sunday afternoon.

On Saturday mid-morning, Paul walked to the back door of his parents' home, knocked, and walked inside.

"Good morning," his mother said. "Hungry? I can fix you breakfast."

"That would be great Mom, thanks. How's Jane doing?"

"She's sleeping," his mom answered. "We stayed up late watching a movie. She's such a treasure."

"I appreciate your help with her, mom. And I'll pick her up tomorrow evening," Paul said.

"She's no trouble. Why don't you just let her stay all week with school being out this week?" his mother asked.

"Well, no. I know you'll be cooking for Thanksgiving and getting food prepared for the church. But, she'll be around," Paul answered. "And you may want to get the food prepared a little early. Have you heard? A big snow storm is headed this way. Supposed to be in here on Wednesday night."

"Good to know and it's good that the church will pick up the food on Wednesday evening," his mother answered.

Paul finished his breakfast and as he was leaving said, "I'll see you tomorrow evening. If you need me, text me. Thanks Mom!"

* * *

Working from home as the early show announcer for the radio station was great for Paul. He was on the air for four hours and didn't have to get Jane out of bed so early; she could sleep in since there was no rush out the door for school.

Everything was working perfectly until Thursday morning, Thanksgiving Day. No matter what Paul did, he couldn't get online with the radio station. He awoke Jane, quickly put her heavy coat on her over her PJ's, and helped her pull on her snow boots.

"Jane, you'll need to walk to Nana's this morning," Paul said in a rush. "I've got to finish getting dressed and out to work. Do you think that you can do that?"

"Yes," said sleepy-eyed Jane. "Pappy and Chief Running Rainbow will help me."

Paul was so frustrated with work, he just ignored the comment. "Oh no. Jane, it's pouring snow! It's like a blizzard. Do you see that outside light on Nana's back porch?" Paul asked holding open the door.

"Yes. I love the snow!" Jane announced and out the door she ran.

The snow was really coming down and was much deeper than it looked. Paul watched Jane as she trenched through the thick, white blanket. Out of nowhere came a blast of wind, blinding him with snow-flakes. Jane disappeared and Paul could not see her. Paul became frantic. He grabbed his shoes, and darted out the door. Suddenly, he saw a glimmer of Jane's arms flying up in the air.

"Jane? Where are you, Jane? I'll be right there!" Paul shouted.

Paul blinked rapidly, but it was still dark and the snow was pounding his face. Paul kept blinking and finally saw Jane in the light of his mother's back porch. Nana opened the door and yelled, "She's here! She's okay!"

Paul ran back inside, grabbed his cell phone, and texted his mom: Heading to the station. Off line. Back soon!

Nana replied: Be careful. Bad roads. Let me know when you get to work.

Paul texted: 4 wheel drive. No problem. Later.

When Paul got to the station, a pre-recorded program was operational. He quickly jumped in and the show never skipped a beat. He finished his work and started home. He texted his mom: Headed Home. Need anything from the store?

His mother texted back: Yes. Milk, eggs, heat up rolls. Ur dad wants red wine. Be careful.

Paul replied: See you soon.

* * *

The snow had stopped and started yet again when Paul arrived home in afternoon. He walked to his mother's back door and knocked. As he stepped inside, he happened to glance down. *What's that?* he thought. He bent over and picked up a colorful feather out of the snow. The feather had all the colors of a rainbow.

"Chief Running Rainbow's feather! I've got to give it back to him," Jane screamed as she ran to the door and reached for the feather.

Paul and his mother exchanged looks. "Maybe it came from one of her toys," his mother said.

"Well, maybe, but she doesn't have a toy with feathers," Paul said handing the feather to Jane.

"It's Chief Running Rainbow's," Jane said.

"Well, since we are on the subject, how did Jane get here this morning with no snow on her boots and no footprints in the snow?" Paul's mother asked in a whisper. "You didn't carry her."

Paul's face turned pale, as if he had seen a ghost. "There were no foot prints in the snow?"

"Pappy and Chief Running Rainbow carried me," Jane said proudly. "They didn't let me get in the snow!"

Paul gave his mother a helpless look, "I'll talk to her later." He changed the subject. "I smell food cooking! And I'm starved," Paul said enthusiastically.

"Yes! Give me an hour or so and we'll sit down and enjoy our Thanksgiving dinner!" his mother said proudly. "You and your dad have a glass of wine while I finish things."

* * *

"Mom, that was that the best!" Paul said taking his last bite of pumpkin pie dessert.

"I agree," his dad said.

"Do you need some help cleaning up, mom?" Paul asked. "It's getting kind of late."

"No. Your dad and I will clean up," his mom answered. "Do you have to work tomorrow night?"

"No. The band doesn't have anything until Saturday night. And hopefully everything will go smoothly with work, because I thought that I'd take Jane tomorrow to see Santa Claus and do some Christmas shopping...providing the weather lets up. So, I'll take Jane home with me tonight. Besides...she and I are going to have a talk," Paul said looking at Jane.

Paul put Jane on his back and carried her home. Jane was quiet and insisted that she carry the feather that Paul found at the back door. Paul opened their front door and set Jane down. She ran to one of the chairs in the living room. She put the feather in the chair. "Chief Running Rainbow will find it here," Jane said.

"Jane, let's get you ready for bed. It's getting late," Paul instructed.

After Jane was bathed, prayers said, and she was tucked in bed, Paul sat down on the side of her bed. "Jane, I don't want to hear you speak of Chief Running Rainbow or Pappy again. Do you understand?"

"No," Jane answered sweetly.

"Because, no one sees them but you. So, no one believes you see them. You do not ever mention them again, or you'll be punished," Paul said harshly. "Do you understand?"

Jane began to cry.

"I love you Jane, but no exceptions," Paul said coldly. He cut out the light and walked out of the Jane's room. It broke his heart to do this, but the time had come for it to stop.

The next morning, the snowing had stopped. His work was executed perfectly, and Paul got Jane dressed so they could go out shopping for the day. By the time they got home, Jane had fallen asleep. Paul tucked her in her bed and said, "Goodnight." As he walked through the living room, he noticed that the feather that Jane had placed in the chair was gone. *Well, mom was here since she left food in the refrigerator,* he thought.

The holidays came and went with lots of family and friends get togethers, band bookings, and work. Soon, Jane was back in school and there was no more mention of Pappy and Chief Running Rainbow.

* * *

Months turned into years and the years passed quickly. Jane had grown into a beautiful young woman. As valedictorian of her high school class, Jane's future was promising. She had been awarded a full scholarship to attend the University of Virginia—Wise, and the family was excited that she would remain close.

"Jane, come on! You're going to be late for your own high school graduation!" Paul yelled from the living room. "And Nana and Papa are on the porch wanting to take your picture! Come on!"

Jane stepped out of her bedroom and walked into the living room. Paul was speechless. "You look just like your mom," Paul said. "You're beautiful!"

Jane smiled.

"Your mom and Pappy would be so proud!" Paul said with tears in his eyes.

Jane stepped out the front door onto the porch when something caught her eye. She glanced down and there was something shining. "Oh look!" Jane said. She bent over and picked up a feather glistening with all the colors of the rainbow.

"Look at all these colors! A feather like a rainbow!" Jane said excitedly.

Paul's mother gasped. Paul and his mother exchange looks of disbelief.

"Chief Running Rainbow must be proud of her too," Paul whispered.

Don't Go in the Cornfield

Jeff Geiger Jr.

It was the last day of eighth grade at the school I attended in Tazewell, Tennessee. I was as ready as a fourteen-year-old kid could be for summer break. After the bell rang I rushed outside, weaving through a throng of school kids, and met up with my friend, Josh. I found him by the school's bike rack.

"You want to hang out at my house?" I asked him as I unlocked my bike. "My mom said it was cool if you ate dinner with us."

"Heck yeah. Can we stop by the comic book store over on Oak Street first?"

"Yeah, sure." I said, throwing a leg over my bike. "Race you there!" I took off down the road, pedaling like a cyclist in the Tour de France.

"Hey, wait up!" Josh said as he mounted his bike.

I looked behind me to see Josh pedaling as fast as he possibly could. He was gaining on me, so I quickened my pace until I created some more distance.

After a minute or two, I glanced behind me to find that Josh was no longer there. I grabbed the brake lever and skidded to a stop. "Josh, Where'd you go?"

I heard faint laughter perhaps thirty yards to my right. It was Josh flying down a dirt road on his Huffy.

I immediately took off after him, but the gap he created between us was nearly the size of an eighteen-wheeler. There was no way I could catch up; although, that didn't stop me from trying.

It was a race downhill to the comic book store. Josh had a good lead, even though he was no longer pedaling. He just cruised down the hill at a good speed because he knew he had me beat. To satiate my competitive side, I didn't just cruise as he was doing; I pedaled as hard as I could, and I went as fast as I ever had on my bike. The wind blew my hair back, and I white-knuckled the handlebar grips as I closed the gap. The store was just fifty yards away now, and the street sign in front of the store acted as our finish line. I made it to his back tire, still gaining speed. As our bikes sped past the street sign, Josh's front tire passed mere inches before mine did.

We each gripped and squeezed our brake levers, sliding our rear tires twenty feet or so until we needed to put our feet down to keep from falling over.

Out of breath, I said, "You know I almost had you, right?"

He smiled. "Maybe next time, Benny."

"Had to cheat, though," I said, elbowing his arm as we parked the bikes next to the comic book store.

"I only took that shortcut because you had a head start."

"Yeah, but—"

"What gives! The comic book store is closed," Josh said.

A sign on the front door read: MOVED TO NEW LOCATION ON BROKEN BRANCH RD.

I read the sign and asked, "Do you know where Broken Branch Road is?"

"Yeah, it's maybe two or three miles from here. Want to go check out the new store?"

"Sure, I just can't be gone too long. My mom will start wondering where I am."

We hopped back on our bikes and rode farther down the road. After a mile or so, we came upon a cornfield on our right.

"That's funny, I don't remember there being a cornfield here," Josh said.

"I wouldn't know. This is my first time out this way," I said.

Josh was leading, since he knew how to get to Broken Branch Road. We were cruising along until I almost ran into his back tire when he abruptly stopped in front of me. "What's wrong? Why'd you stop?" I asked.

"I saw something," he said, looking at the cornfield.

"Saw what?"

He didn't say anything. He continued to stare at the cornfield. All I could see was the back of his head. I asked again. "What did you see, Josh?"

"I thought I saw—there it is again!"

Josh dropped his bike and ran into the cornfield. I watched to see if he'd come back out. After a minute, he still hadn't returned.

"Josh! Come on! I told you I can't stay out late, man!"

Ten seconds or so went by, then I heard, "Benny! Come help, it's going to get me!" I dropped my bike and rushed into the tall field of corn stalks. I pushed my way through, listening for Josh's cries for help.

"Over here, Benny! Hurry, it's got me!"

He was close, but I couldn't tell if the sound came from the left or the right.

"Benny! Where are you!"

This time it sounded as if he were to my left, so I took off in that direction, pushing through corn stalks and trying not to trip. Soon I discovered an open area in the cornfield. It was in the shape of a circle and perhaps ten feet in diameter. On the other side of the circle, I saw Josh lying down in the dirt. His leg was dripping blood, and what wasn't dripping on the ground was running down into his sock. He held his leg up to his chest, breathing rapidly.

"Josh, what the hell, man," I said.

"Careful, Benny, there's something in this cornfield. It looks human but I don't think it is."

"What do you mean?" I asked, walking up to him. "We need to get you out of here. Your leg is bleeding all over the place."

"Yeah, I know."

"Why did you run in here anyway?"

"Because I thought I saw someone."

"Saw who?"

"My grandpa Dan."

"Your grandpa passed away months ago."

"I know, but I swear it was him. It looked just like him, Benny. It's not though. I don't know what it is, but it's not him."

"Can you walk, if I help you up?"

"I'm not sure. That thing cut me with its claws before it let go of me. It was dragging me somewhere, Benny."

"Dude, you're freaking me out. Come on, let's go," I said, and picked him up.

I threw his arm around me and held him tight to my side. I began to walk, and he screamed as soon as he put weight on his wounded leg.

The thing in the cornfield let out a wail. I could hear corn stalks bouncing off its body as it rushed toward us. I picked Josh up, carrying him on my shoulders like a firefighter. As I ran in the direction that I hoped led to the road and back to our bikes, I heard the thing getting closer and closer to us. I felt a hand on my shoulder but tried to keep running. A second later the hand on my shoulder spun me around, and I locked eyes with our English teacher, Mr. Davidson.

"What are you boys doing out here in this cornfield?" he asked.

"It's not him," Josh whispered in my ear. "It's the thing that was my Grandpa Dan earlier. It changed again."

"We were just leaving, Mr. Davidson," I said. "My friend hurt his leg."

"Oh, that's no good. Here, let me have a look."

He reached his hand out toward Josh, but when I saw the incredibly sharp claws on his elongated fingers, I took off running.

"I said let me have a look!" the thing shouted, no longer sounding like our English teacher.

I continued to run, and thought I saw the edge of the cornfield up ahead, but I tripped over a stalk of corn. Josh fell from my shoulders and crashed to the ground. I felt the thing grab my ankle, pulling me back the way I had just come. To my right, I noticed Josh being pulled along with me.

The thing pulling us was no longer our English teacher. It was a boy, perhaps fifteen years old, wearing bedraggled overalls. He was bigger than us in a way that seemed unnatural. He had red hair, freckles, and a feral look about him. His intent was clear, though—he wanted to kill us.

I kicked my foot that was free at his legs and missed a few times before connecting just under his left kneecap. He released me, but not Josh. As I got up, I felt an overwhelming need to run away as fast as I could, but there was no way I could leave Josh behind. I took a deep breath as I ran up and kicked the red-headed boy in his abdomen. The boy's eyes closed as he stumbled back, holding his mid-section. I grabbed Josh, heaved him over my shoulder again, and ran.

"Hurry, Benny, he's running again!" Josh said.

I tried to speed up, but felt my knees begin to buckle with Josh on my back. I could only go so fast; I just hoped it was fast enough.

I could see the edge of the cornfield, but the red-headed kid sounded like he was right behind us.

"Run, Benny, run! He's about to—"

I felt a hard shove just as I was exiting the cornfield. Josh landed on my head as we fell, and everything went black for a little while.

When I woke up, it was dark out. The sun had just gone down and, in the back of my mind, I knew my mom would be worried and angry. Josh lay next to me, waking up about the same time I did.

"You okay, Benny?" he asked.

I looked at my hands, then down at my legs. "Yeah, I think so. What about you?"

"My leg still hurts a lot. It's not bleeding much now, though. Is that red-headed kid gone?"

"I think it was more than just a kid, but it seems to be gone." I sat up and looked around. Our bikes were still there by the side of the road, but when I took a look behind me, the cornfield was no longer there.

"Josh, look. It's gone."

"What's g—whoa! How is that possible? It was right there. We were in there with that thing."

"Yeah, I remember. This is all too crazy. We can think about that later, though. Right now you need to get to a hospital for your leg. Let's get out of here," I said. Josh sat up, grunting in pain.

"I don't know how we're going to get there. I don't think I can ride my—look, a car!" he said, pointing down the road. "Get them to stop, Benny!"

I spun around and saw headlights coming our way. I picked myself up off the ground and stood next to the road, waving my arms in desperation. It wasn't a car; it was an old pickup truck from the sixties. I couldn't see the person driving the truck until I looked through the side window. The old man sitting behind the steering wheel had a badly wrinkled face, a cigar in one hand, and an old trucker cap on his head that said John Deere on it. He shut the truck off and opened the passenger door so we could hear each other.

"You boys okay?" he asked me.

"No, my friend hurt his leg pretty bad. Could you give us a ride to the hospital, please? He isn't able to walk or ride his bike."

The old man jetted smoke from his nostrils after taking a long drag on the cigar. "Yeah, I reckon I could do that. Put them bikes in the bed."

"Thanks, sir," I said, then hurried over to grab Josh and our bikes.

I sat in the middle and Josh sat in the passenger seat, sweating and holding his leg. The old man put the truck in gear and slowly got us moving down the road.

"Now why in the world are you boys ridin' your bikes at night on the side of the road?" the old man asked, not taking his eyes off the road.

"Sir, it'll probably sound crazy, but we got stuck in the cornfield on the side of the road. We were being chased by this *thing* and it tried to kill us!"

"Cornfield? Son, there ain't been a cornfield there since 1972."

"I know it's gone now, but I swear we were in one. We were being dragged by this red-headed kid."

"Red-headed kid, you say? Well, that does make sense. You see, I own that there piece of land where the cornfield used to be. It won't grow crop there anymore, though. Not since that red-headed boy was killed out there in the cornfield. Ever since that day, nothin' would grow. I reckon the soil went sour."

"How'd the red-headed kid die, mister?" I asked.

The old man's lips curled, revealing yellow-rotting teeth as he grinned. "The boy was stealin.' He stole an awful lot of crop from me," the old man said. "Sellin' it behind my back. So I made an example outta him."

My heart was nearly beating out of my chest as I watched the old man drive, frowning thoughtfully at the road in front of him.

"What do you mean?" I said uneasily.

He was still looking ahead when he said, "I mean I killed him. Killed him right where he stood. Shot him with a Smith and Wesson. Crazy thing is, the kid didn't die. His body did, but his soul sure didn't. He even got me back 'bout nineteen years ago. He saw me drivin' down this worn-out road and made the crop appear. I got out of my truck to look at the crop, wonderin' how in the hell it grew back. Then, as I closed my eyes and smelled the corn, he ripped half my face off with those claws of his and pulled me into the cornfield, where he ended my life."

The old man turned to look at me. I hadn't noticed before, but the skin on half of his face was gone.

"If you don't believe me, you can ask him," he said. "He's sittin' right next to you."

I froze for what felt like a whole minute. I didn't want to look. Josh was supposed to be next to me. We were supposed to be going to the hospital to get his leg fixed up.

"Josh?" I said, not looking at the person inches away from me in the passenger seat.

"Yeah, Benny?" It was Josh's voice. I let out a sigh of relief before turning to look at him, except it wasn't exactly Josh. His body was changing into someone else. When I saw his hair change from brown to red, I knew what was happening. I panicked. I reached over the red-headed kid and tried to open the door but it was locked. The red-headed kid pushed me back with his clawed hand and put a slice in my arm six inches long. I felt the truck go off the hard road and suddenly realized the cornfield was back once more. Its stalks seemed to be even taller than before. I turned back toward the old man piloting the truck and at last understood his intent was to take me back into the cornfield, where he and the red-headed kid could murder me. Without hesitation I tried opening his door, but he gripped me by the throat as I pulled the door handle. I was unable to breathe, but I thought he might release me if I jumped out. Even though we were traveling at roughly thirty miles per hour, I didn't think twice about it; I dove out of the speeding vehicle just before the truck entered the cornfield. The old man released the hold he had on my throat, and I rolled in the grass several times before coming to a stop.

My whole body hurt. I had never been in this much pain before. It took me a few seconds to realize that warm blood was running down my arm from the laceration the red-headed kid had made with his razor-sharp claws. I felt like hell, but when I opened my eyes, the cornfield wasn't there anymore. Neither was the old man, the red-headed kid, or the truck.

I attempted to take a deep breath, but agony seized me in the process. I was pretty sure I had broken a rib or two, maybe more. Then I heard a voice say my name. It was a voice I knew.

"Josh?" I said, my voice just above a whisper.

"It's me, Benny."

"It's really you? Not the red-headed kid disguised as you?"

"It's the real me, Benny. I have the cut on my leg to prove it."

I lifted my head with a wince and looked him over. He was using a large stick he found by the road as a cane. His hand was stretched out toward me. I took it, and he helped me stand up.

"How are we going to get home, Josh? Our bikes were in the back of that truck."

"I guess we better get to walking. I don't know about you, but I'm ready to get the heck away from here and never come back."

We walked for maybe two minutes, each of us struggling in a different way, when a police officer pulled up behind us. He must have seen how bad of shape we were in because he flashed his lights and stopped his cruiser next to us.

"My god, are you boys okay? What happened?" the cop asked.

"Not really," I said, showing him my bleeding arm.

"And you wouldn't believe us if we told you," Josh said.

He got out of his car, quickly removing his belt. I wasn't sure why, at first, then I realized he was going to use it to stanch the bleeding. "We'll get the details later," he said, tightening the belt around my upper arm. "Here, take a seat in the back of my car. I'll call an ambulance right now."

A few minutes later, Josh and I were being placed on stretchers. We were loaded into separate ambulances. The paramedics placed me in the back, and one of them said, "You're going to be okay, kid. You're in good hands now." He glanced at the two paramedics up front.

"Okay, guys, he's all yours now," he said, closing the back doors.

The ambulance began to move and I closed my eyes, trying to sleep until this was all over, or at least until we got to the hospital. Then I heard the driver say, "Make sure the kid is strapped down. Don't want him goin' anywhere."

My eyes shot wide open. I knew that voice. The old man that owned the cornfield was driving the ambulance. A moment later, the red-headed kid was standing above me. I tried to get up, but he held me down. I kicked and thrashed around, despite my injured ribs, but it was no use. They had me.

I thought they did, anyway, but it seemed to only be my overstressed brain playing tricks on me. I looked up again and saw that the paramedic did in fact have red hair; although, it wasn't the red-headed kid from the cornfield.

"Calm down, kid," the paramedic told me. "I'm just trying to take your vitals."

I stopped thrashing around and tried to get my breathing under control. "Sorry. I thought you were . . . never mind."

"I'm just here to help, kid." Then he spoke to the driver. "Zach, get us to the hospital. This kid's arm needs stitched up as soon as possible."

"I'm on it," the ambulance driver said.

I felt the ambulance moving. When we got down the road, to the edge of where the cornfield used to be, I looked past the paramedic that was taking care of me. Out of the ambulance's back window, standing on the shoulder of the road was the old man and the red-headed kid. The ambulance's red flashing lights made them visible. The somber expression on their faces conveyed that Josh and I had thwarted them. I watched the old man and red-headed kid turn around, disappearing as they walked onto the vast field of dead grass where the cornfield used to be.

I rested my head, feeling safer now that I was away from them and the cornfield. The paramedic administered something for pain, and I welcomed the relief. I closed my eyes, listening to the sirens wail in the night air as I drifted off to sleep.

HIGHLY RECOMMENDED

LINDA HUDSON HOAGLAND

"Have you been to this place before?" I asked Donna as I pivoted my head to take in all of the strangeness that surrounded me.

"Well, no, but it was highly recommended," she said as she too looked around at her surroundings.

"Who recommended it?" I asked.

"It's someone you probably wouldn't know. The food here is supposed to be really good. They don't serve those tiny, little portions some places call dinner that make you want to find something else to eat as soon as you walk out the door. You know the kind I'm talking about," she said with a sly grin.

"Yes, I do. But—I want to know who recommended it," I said firmly.

"Why does that matter?"

"It doesn't except for the fact that you are trying to hide the name from me. So, tell me," I said as I tried to cover my irritation with a smile.

Donna stared at her lap for a few moments.

"I've got to go to the ladies room. Please excuse me," Donna whispered as she very nearly ran from the table.

I followed her departure from the table with my eyes wide. I was dumbfounded. Why was she acting so silly?

I looked around the small cubicle in which our table was located. Privacy was not an issue in this place with its maze-like interior. When we arrived at the front door, a hostess clad in black led us through dimly-lit, narrow hallways to our cubicle and instructed us to sit.

The hostess had walked so quickly that we couldn't ask questions or look around without losing sight of our leader, who would vanish completely in the darkness in a fraction of a second.

We did as she instructed. We sat.

After catching my breath, I then started the interrogation of Donna until she felt it necessary to run away from my questions.

The little cubicle seemed to be crowding me. I knew it was my mind playing tricks on me. Sitting all alone in dimly-lit silence waiting for Donna's return to the table was wearing on my nerves.

Why on earth would anyone isolate each table so completely from other diners? I wondered. *Why a maze?*

I had no idea how to get out of there. I hoped Donna knew the path. Where was she? Maybe she got lost going to the ladies room. Where was the ladies room? Waiters? Waitresses? Where were they? No one had appeared before me the entire time we'd been seated. It seemed like it had been hours and hours, but I knew it had only been a few minutes.

I had actually thought myself into being afraid. *What should I do?*

"Ellen, I'm sorry it took me so long. It took me a while to find the ladies room," Donna apologized as she seated herself. Her sudden appearance had dragged me from my thoughts of fear.

Instead, my fear was turning to frustration. I could feel the angry tide of adrenaline race through my veins causing my pale skin to flush to a rosy red. I willed myself not to raise my voice, not to say those ugly words that were dancing on the tip of my tongue.

"What's going on, Donna?" I whispered harshly.

"Nothing—nothing at all. Why would you ask me that?"

Again, I was dumbfounded. Before I could conjure up the words to tell her a thing or two, a waiter appeared out of nowhere.

"What would you ladies like to drink?" he asked as he kept his head bowed, allowing no eye contact.

"Iced tea with artificial sweetener and no lemon," I answered.

"Don't you want something stronger?" asked Donna as she contemplated the drinks containing a variety of booze.

"No, I don't think so, at least not right now. I may change my mind later. Right now I want to know exactly what's going on around me," I whispered softly, directing my words toward Donna and away from the waiter.

"I'll have a Tom Collins," said Donna to the hovering waiter who was also clad in the same type of black garb as was worn by the hostess.

"Do you want to order your dinner now?" asked the waiter softly.

"No, not yet," I responded warily.

"Ellen, what is your problem?" asked Donna as she looked into my eyes searching for something. I was not sure what she expected to find written on my irises.

"My problem is you, Donna. What's going on? Why are we at this strange restaurant? Why won't you answer any of my questions?" I could hear the tone of my voice rising to a higher pitch with each question I threw at her.

"Let's order," said Donna as she obviously changed the subject to avoid answering any of my inquiries.

Suddenly, it occurred to me that she might not have the answers.

"Okay, let me look at a menu," I said in a calmer tone as I resigned myself to the idea of her ignorance.

The menu was placed in front of me by the black clad server who must have been standing in the shadows somewhere very close. There were four items on the computer printed piece of cardboard.

"I'll take the special," I said to the waiter. He then promptly shifted his attention to Donna.

"I'll have the same, please," she said softly.

The waiter disappeared around a wall and complete silence blanketed the cubicle. The waiter reappeared quickly with the requested dinners.

"Gosh, that was fast!" I uttered as the waiter placed the serving dishes before the two of us.

The waiter kept his eyes downward, not looking directly at us. The serving dishes, filled with our food selections, looked appetizing and steaming hot. The waiter slipped the bill onto the table next to my plate and brushed his hand against mine causing me to look at him. He kept his steady gaze glued to the bill that was turned face down.

As he stepped away from the table, and before I picked up my fork to spear a piece of the meat that had been cut into bite-sized chunks and smothered in sautéed peppers and onions, I flipped over the bill to see what this meal would cost me.

At the bottom of the bill there was a tiny sized sticky note attached, on which a short word of caution was inscribed

'Don't eat the meat. It could be someone you know.'

"Donna, let's get out of here," I whispered harshly.

"Why, Ellen? Aren't you going to eat your dinner?" she asked as she forked a piece of the meat into her mouth. "This stuff is really good and tender. It's seasoned just right for me."

"Look at this, Donna. Look at this bill right now before you eat any more of that stuff," I said angrily as I thrusted my bill in front of her.

She placed her fork onto her plate and grabbed the bill. She blanched white and immediately rose from her chair, grabbed her handbag, and motioned for me to follow her. I grabbed my handbag and jumped from my chair, knocking it over behind me. I had no idea how to get out of this place. The maze entrance had messed with my internal sense of direction, if I ever had one. I had always told everyone that I could get lost in a brown paper bag. I followed Donna around corner after corner, through the hallways of the maze searching for the door.

"Donna, where are we going?" I whispered loudly.

"I'm trying to get us out of here. I thought I knew the way, but I guess I was wrong," she said softly with a tinge of fear changing her voice to a higher pitch.

"Where are the other people? Isn't anyone else eating? Why don't they have more diners? What kind of place is this?" I demanded in a harsh whisper.

"Ellen, I don't have any answers except that I'm sorry. No one recommended this place to me. I found it on the Internet. It was advertised as an excitingly different kind of eatery with exotic dishes served by handsome waiters who know and understand the meaning of the word discretion—not that we need to be discreet. I had no idea it was this strange," Donna explained hurriedly.

"Okay, okay, Donna, let's just get out of here," I said as I rushed along behind her.

"I'm trying but I've gotten myself all turned around. I guess we'll have to just keep going until we find a door," she said in a tone laced with frustration.

The walls were closing in. I was sure of it. The hallways were suddenly narrower and the lights were dimmer.

"Donna, did you see that?" I asked excitedly.

"What?"

"The walls are moving in and it's getting darker," I answered.

"That's just your imagination, Ellen."

Just to show me nothing was changing, Donna spread her arms out from her sides as far as she could reach and was unable to touch both sides of the hallway because of the distance between walls. She still needed a length of about two more feet to reach to the other wall.

I didn't feel reassured. I knew the walls were moving closer and closer. But why?

"Donna, we've got to get out of here," I muttered.

"I'm trying, Ellen, I promise you that much," Donna said.

We walked on, Donna led the way, but we found no brightly lit 'exit only' signs. We found no doors of any kind, only walls that turned at ninety degree angles leading to nowhere.

I was afraid.

"Donna, maybe we should go back the way we came, retrace our steps to our table, and go from there, again," I suggested.

"If you want to do that, Ellen, we will give it a try. This path is getting us nowhere," Donna mumbled.

I could tell from her trembling tones that she was scared, too.

"Stop a minute, Donna. We need to regroup our thoughts. What do you think that waiter's note meant? What did 'you could be eating someone you know' mean? They can't be cooking human beings, can they?" I asked incredulously.

"I don't know. I don't want to think about that. My stomach lurches every time the idea crosses my mind. I actually ate some of that meat," said Donna as she pressed her hand to her lips trying to stem the flow of the rising gorge in her throat.

"I think that's what he meant. I think he was trying to warn us. I wonder what happened to him. I bet he got into trouble for trying to help us," I whispered.

We both were beginning to feel a little less panicky. Now we could move again. I rummaged in my handbag and removed a red Sharpie.

"I'm going to mark an arrow pointing in the direction that we are walking on each wall each time we make a turn so if we get turned around we will know we've already been here and we won't go in circles in that same direction," I said as I pulled the top from the marker.

"Sounds like a good idea, I think. Let's get going back, I hope to where we started," said a frightened Donna.

I drew a red arrow pointing the way each time we approached a corner. There were plenty of those—arrows and corners.

We continued to walk. I continued to draw arrows, but we never reached the beginning, our starting point, our dinner table on which there was a spread of dining selections not fit for human consumption.

"Donna, how could we not be seeing some of the marks I've already made on the wall? Is someone covering them over as fast as I draw them on? Where did our table disappear to? Did someone take it out of here? How can this building be large enough to house miles and miles of hallway maze? Most importantly, why is someone, or several someones, doing this to us?" I said breathlessly.

We were walking faster and faster and becoming more and more frightened with each step.

"Stop, Donna! Stop!"

"Ellen, we've got to keep going!"

"Why?"

"To get out of here!"

"No, Donna. We need to stay right here and let whoever is doing this to us come to us."

"What are you talking about, Ellen?"

"Well, it seems to me that we are doing just what they want us to do," I said angrily.

"How?"

"We keep walking, and we keep scaring ourselves into a panic state. I think if they want us to play the game that it's their move. What do you think?" I asked as I tried to calm my fear and my temper.

"I don't know anymore. I'm so scared."

"So am I, Donna. So am I."

"What can we do?"

"Sit down on the floor. You sit with your legs stretched out in front of you facing one way and I'll sit stretched out facing the other wall. We will be able to tell if the walls are moving. I truly think they are moving and I want to know how it's being done," I explained.

"It's a good thing I wore pants."

"Pants or no pants, we have to do this," I said.

"I know, I know," Donna whined.

The lights were getting dimmer and the walls started to vibrate.

"Did you feel that, Ellen?"

"I sure did."

"What do you think is happening?"

"I think this is somebody's idea of a joke. Well, I'm not laughing and by the time I get out of here, they won't be laughing either," I said as the anger within me was stirred again.

"Ellen, look at that!"

"What?"

"The wall above your head!"

"What about it?" I screamed as I scrambled around to look behind me.

The wall was fading away like a crumpling piece of opaque cellophane. In its place was a door. I grabbed for the doorknob and turned it, all the while whispering a prayer to get out of this crazy house.

"Let's go, Donna," I shouted and we both scrambled through the door looking like we were being chased by the devil himself.

We were a few feet away on the beautiful path to freedom when the door slammed shut with such force that it surely would have shattered into pieces of splintered wood if it were just an ordinary, run-of-the-mill, front door like the one attached to my house.

We ran to the next street before we realized that we had to go back. Our cars were parked out in front of the building.

"I wish we came to this place in the same car. I don't want to go back there. I should just walk home."

"That's too far to walk and you know it, Donna."

"I know. I just don't want to go back there," she pleaded.

"Neither do I, but we both need our cars for work tomorrow."

"Okay, okay. I just don't want to go through that whole maze again," said Donna.

"We won't. We'll get into our vehicles and get the heck out of there."

We made a quick turn and started walking toward the restaurant of terror.

Two ladies in their late fifties couldn't sneak. That was a fact when both ladies were not the petite tiny size, but instead were the plus and plus-plus sizes that we seemed to have settled into with the advance of time.

When I thought about our attempt at sneaking, I almost broke into raucous laughter at the imagined site of both of us running. We were definitely not gazelles. Whether it was funny or not, we were going to have to get to our vehicles.

"Look at that, Donna. The name of the place is different. Actually there is no name at all. The place looks abandoned and the sign is gone!" I said in amazement.

"Thank, God!"

"What do you mean? I wanted to find out who did this. Don't you?" I stammered.

"No way, Ellen, I don't want anything to do with those crazies. Never again."

"Don't you want to know why they did this to us?"

"No, well, maybe. I want someone else to find out. I'll just go to court and testify," Donna said.

"Testify to what?"

"To what they did to us. What do you think?" Donna said allowing the bottled-up anger to escape into her voice.

"What did they actually do?"

"They fed us human being. They scared us. They wouldn't let us out. I'd say the kidnapped us," Donna said with anger to the point of tears.

"Who?"

"I don't know who."

"How do you know it was human being? Where did it happen?"

"It happened right here. You know it was right here and the waiter told us it was human meat."

"Okay, but now it's gone, isn't it? And, all the waiter said was that it could be someone you know. He didn't actually say it was human being, now did he?"

"No, no, he didn't. It has to be right here. We need to go inside again," said Donna.

"I thought you didn't want to do that."

"I don't, but they've got to pay for what they did," Donna said angrily.

"And what was that?"

"They made me look like and feel like a fool. That ought to be against the law," Donna said as the fight was beginning to drain from her body.

"It's not against the law to make you feel like a fool and you know it."

"What can we do?" asked Donna.

"Until we can find them, we can't do anything. Even if we call the cops when we find them, what can we tell the cops? We only saw the hostess and the waiter. They didn't do anything to us. Did they?"

"No."

"We're going to have to forget about it," I said.

"That's not fair."

"No one said the world has to treat us fairly," I said as I stared at what appeared to be an abandoned building.

"The joke is on us," Donna said as my mind told me to forget about all of it.

My only response was, "I hope I can forget about it."

RAILROAD CROSSING
AN ERWIN TRAIN STORY

COURTNEE TURNER HOYLE

The tired train horn was almost inaudible in the distance.

Samson Hale turned over and tried to go back to sleep, but his bladder threatened to spill. His ritual nighttime trips to the bathroom had started in his sixties, but they had increased in the latter part of his eighties. Katrina hardly stirred anymore when he made his almost hourly treks.

He shuffled from the bathroom to the kitchen, fully awake. He poured a glass of milk, happier for the way it coated his stomach than for the thirst it quenched.

He was tired, but his brain wouldn't shut down and allow him to enjoy the peacefulness of nothing. In his dreams, he could still work with unshaking hands and stand straight as an arrow. When he woke, his joints cried out in defiance of his movements, and it was sometimes a labor to walk from his house to the garage.

He stared out at his neighbors' silent houses. The light flicked on in the Dermont's kitchen. Joe would begin his paper route soon. Lincoln Chamberlain's puppy stirred and yapped at the air. Samson wondered if anyone else was staring out their dark windows, waiting for a new day.

He climbed back into bed as Joe Dermont's headlights flashed across his bedroom walls. Katrina let out a small sound in her sleep, and Samson touched her gently. Her breathing regulated, and she settled into her dreams.

Samson envied his wife's peacefulness. She only slept five hours a night, but her rest seemed uninterrupted. He couldn't lie in bed for more than an hour without the need to relieve himself.

He stayed in bed when Katrina lifted herself from the mattress. She had practiced soft movements that she thought kept him from waking. He loved her for her consideration.

An hour later, Samson sipped on coffee and read the news on his phone. It had been hard to embrace the technology over the feel of the newspaper in his hands, but his grandson had won him over by showing him the way to enhance the words into larger print.

"The town might buy an old train engine for recreational rides," he announced.

"That would be so good," his wife commented. "It would give the community more money and tourism, and it would be fun for us."

"It'd be fun for *you*," Samson grumbled.

"What's that?"

"I can't wait to take you," Samson lied.

"*You* may be burnt out on trains," Katrina huffed, "but the rest of the town loves the idea."

Samson could tell that his wife was ready to have one of her long talks that involved emotion and enthusiasm. "I'm going to go to Willis'," he declared, pecking her on the cheek.

"Will you be back for lunch?"

He shook his head. "That high school kid wants me to meet him at the Clinchfield Drug Store for a quick bite."

"Oh, yes," Katrina remembered.

Samson didn't point out to her that she had suggested the time for the interview. His wife had been more forgetful over the past six months, but every time he mentioned it, she became agitated.

She walked him to the door, wiping her wet hands on a dish

cloth. "You don't have to tell him anything that makes you uncomfortable," she called.

He nodded and backed out of the driveway, pretending to grab the blown kiss she sent at him.

* * *

Willis was already in the middle of a tirade when Samson pulled up one of the metal chairs that lined the walls. Samson watched him with feigned interest. Bo and Bob tried to offer up their comments, but they gave up when they realized that Willis didn't hear them.

Samson had gone to high school with the three men. The four of them had been class clowns, and it was rumored that Bo had been responsible for the bottle rocket that had exploded in the girls' bathroom.

"...and I never hear it," Willis finished.

"Hear what?" Samson asked, pulling up his slacks a little before he sat down.

"The train," Willis said. "Bob has been hearing a train at the same time every night."

Bo and Bob had worked with Samson at the railroad. Bob had been a conductor, and Bo had been an engineer. There were times that the men had worked together on a train, Samson pulling it in front, and Bo and Bob pushing in the back.

"I reckon I heard it too," Samson informed them.

"I've not heard anything," Bo said. "And I'm up all night with my faulty hose."

All the men grunted their sympathy for their shared ailment.

"You'd be able to find the train in the timetables if they still had them," Samson commented.

"Can you find a timetable on your smartphone?"

"No," Willis declared. "The world's gone crazy. Now everything has to be a big secret, so that terrorists won't sabotage a coal shipment."

"You can only find schedules for passenger trains," Bo interjected while Willis readied himself for another diatribe.

"The generations after us had it so easy," Willis began. "They never

31

had to work for anything."

"Now there are a lot of hard workers—" Samson argued, but Willis didn't hear him.

Willis had been a principal for thirty-five years and it had jaded him. Near the beginning of his career in administration, some students tied chairs to the curtains in the eighth-grade classroom and hung them out the windows. After he pulled all the chairs back into the building, he resolved to guide the students with a firmer hand. There were still pranks, but there were stiff repercussions.

"The kids aren't gonna hold up a train," Bo chuckled.

"Where there's a will there's a way," Willis huffed.

Samson quickly changed the subject before his friend continued his rant. "I heard that they're gonna try to renovate an old train car to run passenger rides through town," he told the group.

"I heard it, too," Bo seconded. "They're already working on the engine to pull it."

"Maybe they'll get you to drive it," Willis joked, nudging Samson's knee.

"Very funny," Samson responded, irritated with the comment. He had dutifully navigated the tracks for the CSX Railroad for almost forty years, but he had been retired for a quarter of a century.

The sun climbed high enough for Samson to leave for his lunch meeting. He walked the half block deliberately. When his knees ached or his heart thudded uncomfortably fast, he pretended to stop and look at old signs from dusty decades.

During the time that he had been an engineer, he would have eaten his lunch in the North End Shack, a white building just beyond the CSX office building. Since his retirement, he grabbed a quick meal at the Clinchfield Drug Store when he was in town at lunchtime.

"Grilled cheese and tomato soup," he told Jamie when she waited for his order.

"Good choice," she said, winked at him, and hung his ticket on the rotating order wheel.

Samson scanned the room to see if he had missed the kid from the school's newspaper. When he turned back around, a young man had taken the seat next to him.

"Mr. Hale?"

"The one and only," Samson said, extending his hand, "But you can call me Samson."

"Yes, sir," the teen conceded, but he seemed uncomfortable with the idea of referring to an elder by his first name.

"I'm going to tell you right now," Samson cautioned. "I'm not going to talk about the elephant."

It was well-known that Erwin had been held accountable for the hanging of a circus elephant in 1916. The infamous picture showed a cow elephant hanging by her neck with the railroad's roundhouse in the background. Retellings and rumors had turned facts into mostly fiction, and many of the Erwin residents didn't know the truth surrounding the event. Samson was aware of the particulars of the famous happening, and where the pachyderm had been buried, but he didn't like to talk about the incident. He had a soft spot for animals, and he considered the hanging a dark spot on the reputation of his beautiful county.

"That's okay," the teenager smiled. "I wasn't going to ask you about it. "I'm Peter," he added.

"Well, Peter," Samson said. "What would you like to know?"

Jamie delivered Samson's order, and he realized that he had forgotten to ask for a drink. He ordered two cherry colas and explained to Peter that the drug store still made them by adding cherry syrup. Jamie brought the sodas quickly, and he pushed one of them to Peter. Samson wound his hand in the air, indicating that the boy could begin his interview.

"I'd like to talk to you about Daniel," Peter said.

Samson felt his stomach drop. "Now why would the school newspaper want to know about that?" he responded gruffly.

The man next to him stiffened and turned his head slightly. After a moment, the man resumed chewing and turned in the other direction.

"Did you see him?" Peter asked, ignoring Samson's outrage.

Samson remembered Daniel very clearly. He had been an athletic young man with feathery blond hair and crystal blue eyes. His eyes had haunted Samson since they had closed permanently in October of 1983.

"I see him every night in my sleep," Samson muttered. "I wish I could take his place."

Peter nodded. "Can you tell me about that day?"

Samson stared into his soup, willing it to give him the strength to continue. It was unmoved, reminding him of the blood on the tracks.

"I tried to stop," he whispered. "The police said that he had been camping just outside of the Appalachian Trail. I don't know why he thought it was a good idea to walk on the tracks."

"So, it was *his* fault," Peter concluded.

Samson held his face in his hands miserably and repeated the same thing he had told the police and himself. "He shouldn't have been on the tracks!"

Samson had lost his appetite, so he paid for his meal and left Jamie the usual tip. Peter remained seated when Samson stood from the stool.

"Is that all you wanted to know, young man?"

"That was all," Peter replied. "Thank you for your time."

Samson shrugged. He had expected to discuss his time as an engineer, but the kid had been satisfied with witnessing Samson's breakdown over his biggest regret.

"Are you feeling okay?" Jamie asked Samson. Several people were pretending not to listen to their exchange.

"Chipper as a baby bird," he responded brightly. Abandoning his lunch had not been a great idea, but he had lost his appetite. Katrina would probably hear about it from well-meaning gossipers before he got home. "My eyes were bigger than my stomach," he added, patting his belly.

He rushed out the door, leaving Jamie and the other patrons staring after him.

* * *

Katrina was already peeling potatoes for dinner when he opened the back door. Her potato salad had won prizes in county festivals and it was always a hit at church picnics.

"How did it go?" she asked him.

"He was just rootin' around about the past," Samson replied.

Katrina nodded knowingly. "We all have regrets that we don't want to share with the world," she said. "I miss my sister every day, but I wasn't fast enough to grab her before she fell into the well." She selected another potato out of the bin. "I'm sorry. I thought he was interested in your railroad career."

"I'm not goin' to dwell on it," Samson said proudly. "I left him sittin' at the counter."

"I hope you weren't mean to him," Katrina gasped, pausing a circular cut around a spud. "He seemed like a nice boy."

"He was nice," Samson agreed. "But he was nosy."

Samson and Katrina moved in familiar circles around each other for the rest of the evening. Each of them had their own chores and interests, and they attended to them without the interference of their partner. They met at the table for dinner, made polite conversation, and washed and dried dishes together in silence.

The phone rang just before their favorite game show. Katrina hurried into the kitchen to answer it. She spoke in soft sounds that didn't reach Samson's ears. When she eased into her favorite chair, she seemed distraught.

"What's wrong?" Samson asked.

"Bob had a heart attack," Katrina whispered.

"What?" Samson cried, tightening his grip on the ends of his arm rests.

"He crossed over this evening," she sobbed. Katrina believed that death was simply a movement of the spirit on its way to heaven, so she referred to death as "crossing over." To her, each person's experience was unique to the life he or she had lived. Samson hugged his wife, but he saved his tears for his woodworking room. He heard the phone ring again, but he ignored it.

Samson grieved for his friend privately before he rejoined his wife for bed. Her eyes were red, and her voice was husky, but she didn't mention Bob again.

That night, sleep visited Samson in bursts, filling his mind with vivid images one moment and leaving him in his dark room the next. After a horrifying dream where he relived the final moments before his train collided with Daniel, Samson decided to amble into the kitchen.

His dream had deposited him in the first week of October in 1983. Samson had pulled some coal cars and hoppers to Dante, Virginia. After spending the night at the YMCA, he was placed on a train early the next morning. The fog was thick, and Samson had been working for several days in a row. Bob had been part of the crew, but he was in the back with the flagman. The train had moved carefully, but not slowly enough to warn the tall figure on the track before the train hit him.

Samson sat at the kitchen table, watching the tragic scene from the past play out before him. The memory of the screeching brakes rang in his ears.

He had climbed down from the engine and run to the body thrown down the track, but there was no life in it. Bob had radioed for help, because all Samson could do was stare at the open-eyed young man splayed across the track.

The light flicked on in the Dermont's kitchen, and Lincoln Chamberlain's puppy barked shrilly at the soft glow it cast on the lawn. Samson wondered how many people were awake in his forgotten railroad town.

As if in answer, a train's horn sounded.

* * *

Samson laid down next to Katrina and leaned over to tenderly kiss her head. Her breaths were short, and he wondered if she was awake. When she didn't turn to him or speak, Samson settled onto his side of the bed.

Daniel's death had plagued him for decades, but Peter's questions had spun his guilt to the surface of his thoughts again. Samson hadn't been involved with Daniel's funeral arrangements, but he had built a small, wooden cross for him, and placed it in the field next to the tracks where the young man had died. He used to put flowers beside it on holidays, making a special trip to the site on Daniel's birthday. Sadly, he hadn't visited the cross since he retired.

Samson decided that it might ease his conscience to set fresh flowers by the cross. Perhaps honoring the young man's life by acknowledging the place where it had ended would be enough to help Samson sleep a little better at night.

I'll go today, he resolved, and waited for Katrina to get up and begin their day.

* * *

Samson shuffled up to the train tracks, with chrysanthemums in his hand. The wooden cross he had made for Daniel stood in a field on the other side of the tracks.

A train's horn warned its approach. The wheels crunched the air, sending tiny vibrations up his legs. Gravel shifted behind him, and he wasn't surprised when Peter appeared. Somehow, he knew that Peter had been guiding him here since they met.

"Do you remember him?"

A tear drew a lazy track down Samson's cheek. "He was a young man with a green army pack slung around his shoulder. I only saw the outline of him before I hit him, but he landed face up on the tracks."

"You said it was *his* fault," Peter reminded him.

"That's a lie I told myself," Samson sniffled. "I was getting burned out, and I wanted to go home. I should have been goin' slower."

Samson buried his face in his hands. Sobs echoed off the mountains. When he raised his head, he thought he saw a young man with blond hair and an army pack on the other side of the tracks next to the cross. He shut his eyes tightly to clear his vision.

Peter was staring at him when he opened his eyes. "This can be your train if you choose it," Peter offered.

There were so many reasons for Samson to stay. He had a loving wife, great friends, and a good community, but his life wasn't the same as it had been when he was a young man. Aches and pains plagued him every day, and short walks threatened to send him to the hospital. He wondered how long it would be before he became a burden to Katrina and their children.

The commanding locomotive materialized. It was only carrying a few empty coal cars, but it needed an engineer. Somehow, Samson knew that Bob was in the back with the flag man.

Samson decided that he was ready. He blew a kiss in Katrina's direction, and stepped onto the track. The horn blew its forlorn cry as the train bore down on him, extinguishing his life, and releasing his guilt.

After the engine disappeared, a young man emerged. He reshouldered his army pack, crossed over the track, and continued on his way.

* * *

Katrina held their wedding picture in her hands. She had carried it with her to the funeral, hugging it when she wasn't looking at it.

Night was closing in on the house, but she didn't want to turn on a light. Lights signaled life inside a house, and she didn't feel alive. Her sweet husband was gone, and he had left her behind.

Bob's wife had offered to stay with her. They both had endured similar tragedies, but Katrina had sent her home. She preferred to be alone with her grief.

She had no clear memory of the passage of time as she sat on the couch. She stared at the blank television. Sometimes she wiped tears from her face.

Finally, she moved to the bedroom. Her friends wondered how she could sleep in the same bed in which her husband had crossed over. The answer was easy—the brain aneurysm had taken him immediately, pulling his spirit from his body swiftly. If any part of her husband lingered, then she wanted to be close to it.

On the morning he had died, she had not felt him stir for hours. He didn't know that her sleep had been abbreviated for almost a decade. She let him have his nighttime roamings through the house, and he allowed her to have peaceful moments in the kitchen before he officially rose for the day. They had the perfect schedule, a compliment of each other.

She had been concerned when his eggs and bacon had gotten cold that morning. She wondered if he was sick, and then she had debated if the things she had heard were true. *Had he been talking to himself in town?*

Jamie had called her when Samson had hurried out of the drug store. He had been talking to himself, and some of the patrons had been scared. She had assured Jamie that everything was okay, but when the boy from the school newspaper had told her that Samson had missed their meeting, she had been anxious. *Could he be in the early stages of dementia?*

She had crept to the room slowly, deliberately placing her feet on the boards that didn't creak. Samson had lain in the same position. She had watched for his chest to move, but she didn't see it.

"Samson!" she had cried out, running to the bed and shaking him. One eyelid had revealed part of his eye, but he had been unresponsive.

Katrina had known he was already gone, but she still dialed emergency services. They had pulled into her driveway with blaring sirens. They had left in silence.

She settled onto the pillow and breathed steadily. She thought about her loving years with Samson and was grateful for the time she had shared with him.

Sleep enveloped her and she was swallowed by a nightmare. She drifted out of her body and stared as her husband's breath stopped. She watched herself lay on the other side of him with her eyes open, oblivious to his crossing. Her bedroom faded and she was picking flowers in a field by a well. She watched as her sister balanced around the tip of the well. She looked like a bird, with her arms outstretched and her hair whipping in the wind.

Suddenly, her foot slipped, and Katrina ran for her. She was helpless when her sister's head bounced off the rock around the well and her body folded before it fell into its depths.

Katrina's eyes popped open. She was thankful for the break in her dream, even if it meant she had to face the darkness alone.

She pulled the wedding picture from her chest and blew a kiss at the man who had stood with her on that day and every day after that for sixty-seven years. She missed him so much that pains tugged at her heart.

Lincoln Chamberlain's puppy yapped at an imagined threat. She breathed in the silence and waited for Joe Dermont's lights to wash over her bedroom wall.

Deep in the stillness of the night, she heard a lonesome train horn.

Courtnee Turner Hoyle acknowledges contributions from Edward Williams and Martha Erwin. These individuals related information that allowed her to expand on details about trains, CSX occupations, and regular CSX routes.

OLD MAN DAN

JEFF GEIGER JR.

("Old Man Dan" is a sequel to "Helen's Hill," a story published in
These Haunted Hills: A Collection of Short Stories Book 2)

It had been exactly one year since Brent Ackerman was buried alive on Helen's Hill. Old Man Dan, the barkeeper, had warned the young man of the notorious Kentucky hill and its danger. He even told Brent the story of how Helen was killed by a drunk driver on that very hill; it was right after she married the love of her life. A drunk driver swerved into the married couple's lane, causing a head-on collision as they were leaving for their honeymoon. Old Man Dan informed the young man, but he traveled over the hill anyway. He remembered reading about Brent in the Perry County newspaper, and how he wished the kid would have heeded what he told him that night. Old Man Dan warns almost everyone that comes in the bar about Helen's Hill, especially on the same night she was killed all those years ago.

It was almost two in the morning, and everyone had left the bar. Old Man Dan was getting ready to close the place and finished up by giving the countertop one last wipe down. As he went to grab some cleaning supplies from under the counter, he heard a man's voice; one that was vaguely familiar. Except the man's voice sounded raspy this time.

41

"I'll take a whiskey, splash of Coke, please," the man said.

Old Man Dan froze under the counter, wide-eyed. The voice and drink order engendered a harrowing thought. "Ain't no way that's him," he whispered.

"Are you still open?"

Old Man Dan closed his eyes and stood up. When he opened them, he didn't see anyone. Then to his left, he heard the voice again. "Whiskey, splash of Coke, please."

His eyes shifted in the direction the drink order came from and saw the ghost of Brent Ackerman sitting at the bar, the man who had been murdered by Helen precisely one year ago.

Brent didn't look like your stereotypical ghost, though; this ghost wasn't transparent. His skin was livid with dark purple veins that bulged from his face and body.

"How," Old Man Dan said. "This ain't possible. You died on that hill. I read 'bout it in the paper."

"But they never found my body, did they?"

"No. From what I heard, they didn't."

"That's because it's buried on that hill. Her hill."

"Why are you here? You ain't got no business bein' here," Old Man Dan said, breathing heavily.

"Don't fall out on me, old man. I came here to help you," Brent's ghost said.

"Help me how? By scarin' me half to death?"

"Look, Old Man Dan, have a drink with me and I'll tell you why I'm here. Okay?"

"Then you'll leave and never come back?"

"Sure, old man. Sure."

Old Man Dan reached under the counter and grabbed a bottle of whiskey, pouring a little in two separate glasses. He handed Brent a glass and took a sip out of his own before saying,

"We're out'a Coke."

"That's okay. I can't taste much these days anyway," said Brent's ghost.

"Now tell me what'n the heck is goin' on."

Brent gripped the glass of whiskey and downed it. As Brent was drinking the alcohol, Old Man Dan noticed Brent's hands and forearms were covered in dirt, as if he had clambered out of his grave only a minute ago. Brent raised the empty glass in front of him and smacked his lips together. After setting it down, he leaned on the bar and looked Old Man Dan in his rheumy eyes. "I should have listened to you that night. You were trying to help me, but I thought you were full of it. So now I'm here to try to help you."

The old man's brow furrowed. "Go on."

"Helen knows that you've been warning people about her and the hill. She knows that you warned me and many others, and she's not happy. Not happy at all. I don't know how but she's getting stronger. She wants you dead, old man. I knew I had to sneak away, if only for a few minutes, to warn you. If she caught me here, I'd be worse than just dead."

Old Man Dan raised the glass of whiskey to his mouth, but had trouble drinking it with his hand shaking so badly.

"That damn woman has taken enough lives on that hill. Of course I'm gon' warn people 'bout her. It ain't like she can reach me all the way over—"

Lightning struck and the lights in the bar flickered three or four times before finally going out.

"You still there, Brent?" Old Man Dan asked.

"I've got to go," Brent's ghost whispered. "I think she's here."

"No, don't go! Don't go!"

It was too late. When Old Man Dan lit a candle, he saw that Brent was gone. The glass Brent drank the whiskey out of rested on the bar where he left it. He looked toward the door and now heard rain pounding on the bar's metal roof. After another bolt of lightning flashed outside, the bar's lights began to flicker again, creating a strobe-light effect. Old Man Dan walked over to peek out of the tinted front windows. It was difficult to see much with the bar's sign out front flickering on and off. At first, he saw nothing. Then, after another flash of lightning, something appeared in the middle of the road. It was lying down flat on its back.

Old Man Dan had a good idea of who was in the road, but he couldn't move his feet. He watched as the dark figure slowly sat upright. A few seconds later, its head quickly shot toward the bar and Old Man Dan fell over in fear as he locked eyes with Helen, the woman that haunted the deadliest hill in Kentucky. He got up as quick as his arthritic joints would allow and shuffled over behind the bar, reaching for the shotgun that he kept under the counter in case of an emergency.

"This ain't happenin'. I must be losin' my damn mind," he said to himself. "I ain't even on her damn hill."

There was a *thud* on the front door. It sounded as if someone had thrown their body against it.

"Go away!" Old Man Dan said. "I didn't run you off the road all those years ago! Go find someone else! Leave me be, damnit!"

He sat on the floor behind the bar and racked the shotgun, inserting a shell into the chamber. "If you try to come in here, I'm gon' blast you back to that hill of yours!"

The front door flew open with so much force that it broke the top and bottom hinge, causing the door to lean badly. Old Man Dan peeked over the countertop to see a dark figure in a dress by the entrance. She was drenched from the rain and her wet hair clung to her face. He ducked back behind the bar and could hear her wet feet plopping on the tile floor as she took slow steps toward him. He aimed the barrel of the shotgun under the counter where he saw her last and squeezed the trigger. His ears began to ring, and the recoil from the buttstock left him with a dull pain in his shoulder. That pain was far back in his mind though. He was trying to listen for Helen, but his hearing had not come back just yet.

Old Man Dan racked another shell into the shotgun's chamber. He couldn't remember how many shells the gun held at that moment, but he wanted to say four. After a solid minute of aiming the shotgun's barrel above the countertop from the floor, his hearing began to come back.

He heard the rain starting to die down outside and thought that maybe he had shot Helen. He was about to stand up and look around to confirm this when something occurred to him—*Would a gunshot even kill her? She's already dead after all.*

He looked anyway.

He didn't see Helen or her body anywhere. Then he felt something wet on his head. A drip of water. Then a few more drips, followed by several more. Old Man Dan glanced up to find Helen glowering at him, her back against the ceiling as if she were glued to it. He fell against the floor, knocking the wind out of himself, and fired twice at Helen.

After the second shotgun blast, the lights inside of the bar stopped flickering and stayed on. Helen was gone once more. Old Man Dan waited until his breathing became somewhat normal before he got up to his knees. He listened closely for any sounds that could indicate Helen's presence, but the bar was completely quiet. He rose shakily to his feet and racked the shotgun again, just in case. He felt in his pocket for the key to his Ford pickup; it was still there.

"Time to get the hell out'a this place before she comes back," Old Man Dan muttered, and then the back door to the bar creaked open.

"Come on, old man, this way." It was Brent's ghost.

"Son, am I glad to see you."

"No time to talk—she'll be back soon," Brent said as he waved him over.

Old Man Dan shuffled to the back door and closed it behind him, not bothering to lock it.

"What do we do?" Old Man Dan asked.

"You have the key to your truck?"

"Right here in my pocket."

"What are you waiting for? Get in your truck and drive as fast as you can in the opposite direction of that hill."

Old Man Dan nodded. "I hope you find peace, son. I really do."

Brent's ghost smiled and disappeared.

Old Man Dan dug the Ford key out of his pocket and ran faster than he had run in years toward his truck. He felt immense bone on bone pain in his knees as soon as he took off. His teeth were clenched tight, and by the time he reached the driver-side door of his truck he was gasping for air. As he reached for the door handle, he felt the shotgun being ripped out of his other hand. Then a hard blow to the back of the head, followed by darkness.

He awoke in the front seat of his truck, his head throbbing as it rested against the passenger side window. He realized his hands had been tied behind his back with some kind of rope, and that he had been seat-belted in so that moving from the passenger side would be nearly impossible. The most disturbing aspect of Old Man Dan's situation was the person he saw behind the wheel of his truck.

"Brent? What you doin'?"

"Helen's orders. Sorry, old man."

"You—you tricked me!"

Brent grinned, steering wheel in one hand, Old Man Dan's shotgun in the other. "It's not so bad on the hill, you know. You get used to being dead."

Old Man Dan struggled in his seat and kept working on getting his hands free. "Killin' me ain't goin' to change anything. I don't know what she promised you but—"

"We're here," Brent said, putting the Ford in park. "Time to show you your new home, old man."

Brent pointed to the field of crosses on the side of the road and chuckled at the terrified look on the old man's face. Brent smirked before getting out of the truck to walk around to the other side, leaving the shotgun in the front seat. When Old Man Dan noticed he left the shotgun, he hit the lock on the door with the side of his head so Brent wouldn't be able to get in on the passenger side. Then, Old Man Dan felt the rope loosen as he finally got the knot to come undone. With his hands free, he removed his seatbelt and shifted to the driver's seat, lifting the shotgun and aiming it at Brent's ghost. But Brent only smiled.

"Are you going to shoot me and leave, old man? If so, don't you need this?" Brent said, holding the Ford key up.

Old Man Dan squeezed the shotgun's trigger and the passenger-side window shattered. Brent disappeared just as Helen had at the bar earlier that night. Old Man Dan racked the shotgun before getting out of the truck, keeping the gun leveled as he exited. The yellow glow from the Ford's headlights was the only source of light he had at the time, but it was enough to see the truck key lying on the ground next to where Brent's ghost had been moments ago. He bent down to pick it up, his ears still ringing from shooting the gun. As he gripped the key, the hair on the nape of his neck stiffened. He felt someone behind him. Briskly, he spun around and trained the shotgun at Helen, squeezing the trigger to only hear a click; the shotgun was out of shells, and Old Man Dan was out of luck.

Helen grabbed the barrel of the gun, ripping it out of the old man's hands. "You will stay on this hill with the others. You may resist if you must, but it is futile," Helen said, then hurled the shotgun deep into the woods. "In the end, they all come to realize that this is their home. You will too."

"Not goin' to happen, you damn—"

Old Man Dan felt a dozen hands grip him from behind. The trapped souls of Helen's Hill wrestled him to the ground, holding him there. Helen ambled over, picking up the key to Old Man Dan's truck, and got behind the wheel of the Ford. She inserted the key into the ignition, turning it until the truck fired up. Old Man Dan lay on the pavement, the trapped souls of Helen's Hill laughing hysterically as they pinned him down. Helen revved the engine and put it in reverse.

Brent materialized next to the other trapped souls and helped hold Old Man Dan down.

"Don't worry, old man, it'll be over before you know it," Brent said.

And Brent was right.

Helen mashed the accelerator down and the tires chirped as they gripped the asphalt. Old Man Dan gave it everything he had to get away, but it was no use. With the side of his head resting against the asphalt, he watched as the driver-side rear tire rolled toward him.

"Let me go, damnit!" Old Man Dan said, the tire inches away from his face. "Let me—"

And before the darkness took him, Old Man Dan saw two things — the tire, of course, and Helen's face in the truck's side mirror, her lips spread into a smile.

SOMETHING WASN'T RIGHT

LINDA HUDSON HOAGLAND

The hair on the back of my neck stood straight up as I entered the grocery store. I wasn't sure what was about to happen, but I knew something wasn't right.

I've always tried to pay attention to my gut feelings that caused such a reaction. In order to pay heed to the advice of my gut, I looked around with a fiercely critical eye. I saw neighbors doing the same task of shopping for dinner, but they didn't acknowledge me even though I raised my hand in friendship. They were so focused on getting the necessities and checking out so they could leave.

How weird, I thought. I grabbed a few items that were on my list and continued my intense observations.

"Hi, Martha," I shouted to a friend turning into the next aisle.

When I received no response, I walked hurriedly to catch up with her. When I was rolling my cart along beside her I said, "What's happening?" It was the normal salutation my friends and I would share.

"Oh, Ellen, I can't talk now. I'm in a hurry," she said. She took off running to the cash register.

What is going on with these people?

I dropped a couple more items into my cart and walked to the back section of the store where the refrigerated meat was sold.

Oddly enough, no one else was there perusing the meats. I glanced at what I thought was a roast and noticed that it didn't look like beef or pork. When I moved closer to read the label, I got a whiff of a peculiar smell. It didn't smell like any cows or pigs that had been proportioned for sale.

BUTT ROAST - ABEL JOHNSON

I read the label again. I was sure I had made a mistake. Nope — no mistake. I looked at the next labeled package.

SHANK ROAST - SARAH MEADE

That can't be. I know Sarah Meade. Maybe they are telling me she prepared it for sale.

I walked a little further and came upon a label that read, BABY TOMMY SMITH - LEG QUARTERS

I turned immediately and fled the store leaving my cart standing in the middle of the aisle. When I reached the fresh air outside, I took a deep breath and released it very slowly as I fought back the gorge that was rising into my throat.

I was in desperate need of groceries, so I drove to the next small town on Route 19 that was about twenty miles away from my home.

As soon as I arrived home from my food shopping I called my neighbor, the one who had ignored me when I saw her earlier in the day.

"Annie, what is going on at the grocery store?" I asked as soon as she said hello.

"What do you mean?" said Annie. She was trying to act like she didn't know what I was talking about.

"You know what I mean," I snapped back at her. "I'm sure you went to the meat section and read those labels just like I did."

"Well, yes, I did. Did you read those labels the same way I did?" asked Annie in a voice that told me the idea scared her.

"I thought it was carved up people parts. Is that what you thought it was?" I asked in a voice barely above a whisper.

"It really can't be that, can it?" she responded in a whisper.

"I certainly hope not but I'm really afraid it might be," I said conspiratorially. "I'm going to call Martha and see what she thinks. I saw her there today and she looked startled and confused, which is what I too felt when I left the store."

"Call me back if you find out anything," said Annie before she disconnected the call.

I didn't want to believe what Annie and I were thinking. Maybe it was someone's idea of a joke. If so, it was certainly a sick joke.

I decided my next step would be to call the police department. I wanted to know if anyone else had reported the problem.

"Stillwell Police Department, how can I help you?" asked a cheery, young voice.

"I'm Ellen Harris and I want to know what's going on at the grocery store?" I asked shyly. I was afraid the cheery, young voice might tell me it was nothing and that no other calls had been received.

"No one has called. Would you be able to come to the police station and talk to the detective?" she asked as if she were reading it off of a piece of paper.

"Why? If no one else has reported a problem, why would you need to speak with me?" I asked apprehensively.

"It's very important. You just need to come in here to talk with the detective," she said encouragingly.

"Okay. I'll be there in a little while," I answered, skeptical.

As soon as I disconnected that call I dialed Martha's number.

"Hey Martha," I said excitedly. "What did you think of the meat sale at the grocery store?"

"It made me sick. I had to leave. I'll never shop there again even if I have to drive twenty miles to do the grocery shopping."

"I called the police department and they want me to go down there to talk to them. I'll find out what this is all about for the both of us," I told Martha.

"Let me know what's going on. I will do my shopping elsewhere until this gets cleared up. I may not shop there ever again," said Martha in a determined tone.

I wondered why I was the only one to call the police department. On second thought, of the three of us, I was the only one that would make waves. No one else would speak up.

Let's get this over with.

I returned to my car and headed for the police station.

"Hi, I'm Ellen Harris. I called you earlier about the problem at the grocery store. I am supposed to talk with a detective," I said with trepidation. I was not at all sure I was doing the right thing.

I was led into what looked like an interrogation room where several people were standing or sitting as I entered.

"Ms. Harris, have a seat, please," said a man who dressed in a suit and tie.

"What's going on here?" I asked with concern.

"What did you want to say about the grocery store?" asked the suited man whom I presumed to be the detective.

"You know my name which is Ellen Harris for the rest of you who might not know. Now, tell me who you are and who are all of the rest of these people," I said.

"My name is Jeremy James and the rest of these people are with the production company for *Who Would Have Thought*, the television show that will air for Halloween. I'm not going to introduce each one of them to you, because you probably won't remember the names. I have trouble remembering them sometimes myself."

"Really," I said displaying a lot of skepticism.

"Have you returned to the grocery store since your initial visit?" he asked.

"No, I'm not sure I ever will," I answered angrily.

"Why would that be, Ms. Harris?" he asked.

"They were selling people's body parts as food to eat! I will not go back," I sputtered.

"If you return to the grocery store, you will find that that is no longer happening. It was a Halloween test to see how people would react. Others walked away but you were the only one to take action by calling the police," Jeremy explained.

"This was a joke? A prank for Halloween? You are truly sick people," I said angrily.

"We would like you to sign a release so we may use your reaction on the program," Jeremy said.

"No, never, and I hope you know you have ruined the business at the grocery store. All of my friends will see to that. They never should have let you do this," I said as I walked out of the room.

The Patterson Family that owned the grocery store had to sell the business because of the decline of customers. I was sorry to see the Pattersons leave town but a new, big box chain store moved into town and took over. Maybe it was a good Halloween trick for the residents of Stillwell.

THE HOUSE REVISITED

BEV FREEMAN

("The House Revisited" is a sequel to "The House," published in
These Haunted Hills: A Collection of Short Stories Book 2)

Months passed before Breanna and Lauren chanced going past the old cemetery or even near the house. One fall day, the sun felt exceptionally warm and all the leaves radiated colorful glory. They walked aimlessly on forested trails, Lauren snapping photos of red and yellow maples, the lime green hue of a Walnut, and the lovely golden hickory and oak trees. Soon, the trail crossed a creek, causing the girls to question their location.

"I think this is Buffalo Creek that runs by the old cemetery," Breanna said. "We're close to the plantation."

"My history teacher says someone bought the place and they're renovating it for a Bed & Breakfast," Lauren told her. "I never want to stay there. You?"

Breanna shook her head and said, "Those are pecan trees, part of the grove on the back side of the house. We approached from a different direction."

"Let's not go any closer," Lauren caught Breanna's arm.

"I wonder if it looks different?" Breanna pulled free, moving toward the trees.

Lauren followed, keeping her friend in sight. Breanna moved quietly, stopping behind one of the old growth pecan trees. Lauren crouched behind a scrub oak.

Breanna motioned. "Come see what they're doing!"

"No! You come here!" Lauren whispered.

Breanna ignored caution, moving to another tree, and then another, until she was out of Lauren's sight.

Lauren waited for what seemed like an hour. The sun dropped low in the sky. Soon Buffalo Mountain would rob the daylight. Lauren worked her way around to the front of the property. At least she knew her way home in the dark if Breanna didn't show soon. Suddenly, Lauren felt relieved to see Bree coming from the front gate straight toward her.

"I've been talking to the caretaker, Mose. He's very nice, and invited us back to meet the new owners. They're in Asheville today." She brushed past Lauren saying, "We should hurry. It'll be dark soon."

At the end of the dirt lane, the rickety old bridge looked shakier than ever. Lauren stopped. "Bree, this isn't safe anymore. I'm going through the creek." She jumped to a large rock in the edge of the water, and then leapfrogged across the shallow stream climbing the bank on the other side.

Breanna continued, choosing her steps carefully until Lauren heard a loud crashing sound. She turned to see Bree fall; rotten boards collapsing around her.

"Bree!" Lauren ran to Breanna. "Can you hear me Bree?"

A voice from behind her said, "That ol' bridge finally gave way, huh?"

Lauren turned to see an old man with a white beard looking down at Breanna.

He moved closer and put his hands under the girl's shoulders, "You get her legs and we'll lift her out. She's just got the wind knocked outta' her."

As soon as they lifted her up, Breanna sucked in a deep breath.

"See, just needed them lungs opened up!" The old man carefully set her down in the tall grass on the creek bank. "Sit here till your head stops swimming."

"What?" Breanna said.

"The bridge fell, and you with it," Lauren said. "Where do you hurt?"

"My entire body," Bree tried to laugh. "Oh, that hurts."

"I'm calling Blake. He'll pick us up." Lauren put her phone back in her pocket. "Say! Where did Mose go?" She turned in a circle looking for him, "He helped me pull you out, and now I can't see him anywhere."

Soon, Blake's truck skid to a stop at the site of the bridge. He jumped out and slid down the creek bank to where his little sister lay. "What are you two doing here anyway?" He didn't give them a chance to answer. He lifted Breanna in his arms and climbed into the truck, setting her on the passenger seat. "Come on, Lauren," he ran to the driver's side and got in.

"I'm here." She slammed the door.

Breanna insisted on showering and washing her hair before she went to bed. Blake said their parents were staying in Knoxville for an early meeting tomorrow. So Lauren asked her parents if it was ok that she stay with Bree. Her folks agreed, and Lauren told Blake she'd watch out for Bree.

That's when he pressed the issue of why they were at of the old plantation in the first place. Laura explained about hiking the trails and ending up in a place they hadn't been before. She told him of Bree going to the house and meeting Mose, the caretaker.

"Wait a minute. Mose? The old, black caretaker with the beard?" Blake asked.

"I guess it was him. He looked like Uncle Remus, just like Bree described." She scratched her head, "He disappeared after helping me move Bree." She and Breanna headed upstairs before Blake could ask any more questions.

The next morning Blake let the girls sleep late; they'd had a rough day on their misadventure.

Lauren awoke first and found Blake in the kitchen. "Bree had a rough night, must have had nightmares. She's resting now." Lauren sat on a stool.

"What possessed you girls to go up there anyway?" Blake asked. He poured a glass of orange juice handing it to her.

"We didn't plan it. The leaves were pretty and I was taking pictures. It wasn't until we came to this great big pecan tree that I realized where we were!"

"Pecan trees, in this part of Tennessee?" Blake grinned. "Were there pecans on it?"

Lauren nodded her head. "Honest, Blake. They are huge pecan trees. I was surprised, too."

"I'm going to have to see that!" He punched her gently in the arm and left the room. "I've got some work to do. Don't let Bree sleep too much."

Bree came into the kitchen as Lauren finished her juice. "Want some?"

Breanna slid a stool close to Lauren's, "What I need is coffee to make my head stop hurting."

The girls perched on the stools talking about what happened. Lauren was still concerned about not thanking Mose for his help. Breanna was sore all over and had nasty bruises. However, she felt lucky not to have been hurt worse.

The following week was Fall Break for all the city schools. Blake suggested the girls show him the so-called pecan tree. So, as soon as each one had done the chores their parents assigned, they set off pecan tree hunting.

The shortest route was up the lane from the collapsed bridge. Choosing their steps carefully, the trio crossed Buffalo Creek and walked the seldom traveled road toward the plantation. As they drew closer, Bree wedged between Blake and Lauren, claiming to feel a chill in the air.

No car in sight—they thought if anyone was there they must be parked around back. Having no idea who the new owners might be or if they were welcome, Lauren felt strange walking on the property.

As they passed the old entrance to the basement, Blake pointed out there was a new opening. "Someone opened up the basement," he said.

Around back they saw no vehicle or signs of anyone, but they heard sounds coming from within the house. Blake said "Well, the power is on, something's changed."

"We came to see the trees, they're further back there," Lauren pointed toward a tall canopy of mature trees. They approached and sure enough, there were three trees and nuts all over the ground.

"We need something to put these in. That's a lot of pecans!" Blake said. "I'll look for a basket or something, and ask permission if I find anyone."

The girls gathered a pile of nuts, but Blake hadn't returned. They went looking for him. The door to the kitchen stood open. Bree called out, "Blake!"

The door slammed shut! Both girls jumped, grabbing onto each other.

Blake walked from around the basement side of the house, "Found one," he held a rectangular peach basket over his head. "What's the matter? You two look like you've seen a ghost."

"The kitchen door was wide open," Bree said, still holding onto her friend. "And then it slammed shut, bam!" Her whole body shivered.

Blake looked to Lauren, "For real? Because it was closed when I walked past going to the basement."

"I don't think we should take the pecans. If someone has bought the place, we'd be stealing," Lauren said.

"That's why I'm going in." Blake went to the door, knocked, no response, so he tried the handle. It opened and inside he went.

Again, the door slammed shut!

"Blake!" Both girls yelled. Lauren broke free from Bree's hold and ran to the door. She tried the knob. It didn't budge! "Someone's holding it! Blake!"

Breanna joined her. Together they pushed the door until it opened. Lauren stepped in first, closely followed by Bree. They saw no one, heard nothing, but smelled an awful stench.

"What's that smell?" Breanna asked, clasping her hand over her nose and mouth. "Some kind of chemical?"

"Cover your face. It might be caustic," Lauren pulled the neck of her shirt up over her mouth and nose. She walked into the dining room. Still no Blake. She pushed herself, scared, but knowing Blake was alone and she had to help him. Bree was right behind her. There was no sign in the living room either. They turned and started upstairs. Lauren hugged the wall. Bree hugged Lauren. Both felt their hearts pounding, but they kept going.

The staircase curved right as it climbed, blocking their view of the landing below. Lauren paused, but chose to go on. At the top she looked left around the wall. Nothing but a closed door at the end of the hall. To the right we're several doors, all closed. The smell faded a bit. Lauren and Bree tried the handle of the first door, it opened to reveal an empty room. The next door was the same. Door number three wouldn't open. Lauren knocked lightly, but no answer.

They heard the roar of a motor shutting down. The last door opened on its own. The room was dark, no sunlight from windows, if it had any. Lauren told Bree to use her phone's flashlight to look around, but shining the tiny light in the darkness didn't show them much. They could tell it was not empty, but it was not really clear what objects were in the room. Everything was covered with black, draped material.

Some unidentifiable sound caused Bree to glance behind them at the other end of the hall. Light shone under the door and the smell became strong again. "We should check that room," Breanna pointed.

Lauren nodded. They walked down the hall to the first door. She tried the handle. "Locked," she whispered.

At the same time, Breanna felt a hand on her shoulder and she screamed! Lauren was startled; she screeched, spinning around to see what the situation was. "Blake! What the heck?"

Laughing at their reaction, he said, "It's me, what are you scared of?"

"Why are you slipping around?" Breanna hit her brother's shoulder with her fist. "You scared the mess out of me."

He laughed again, "Come on, I'll explain." He turned and bounced down the steps.

The girls followed him, happy to see he was not in danger like they thought.

Outside, Blake began, "Well, in the first place, that smell is furniture stripper. It can burn your lungs, so I had to get you out of there. Secondly, you did not see Mose, he died in the early nineteen hundreds. The Uncle Remus guy you described is Samuel, hired by the new owners to refinish all the woodwork. When the chemical odor reaches a certain level, the exhaust fan in the attic kicks in, causing the doors to slam as it pulls the stale air out."

Lauren smiled at Breanna and shrugged her shoulders. "I feel silly, how about you?"

"You're the one that wanted to rescue Blake." Breanna folded her arms across her body. "I wasn't letting you go in the house alone."

"Thanks, both of you. Good to know you had my back," Blake said. "Now let's go pick up some pecans. We have permission."

"Whose permission?" Lauren asked.

"Samuel, the new caretaker."

Blake dropped the basket beside the pile of pecans. "Let me see if I can shake the tree." After a couple hard stomps against the tree's trunk, nuts fell all around them.

On their way home, Bree and Lauren discussed uses for the pecans.

"I'll shell the nuts if you promise to make at least one pie." Blake moved between the girls, "It's very nice to have two sisters."

Lauren said, "It's nice to have a big brother. I'm not an only child anymore."

For a few days the girls didn't think about the house. Lauren's Mom helped her make three pecan pies. One for Blake, one for Samuel, and the other for their own family.

As soon as the pies cooled, Lauren walked the block to Bree's house.

"That smells yummy," Bree said. "I hope I get a piece before Blake gets back."

"Aw, Blake's not here? I wanted him to go with us to the plantation house. I made a pie for Samuel too."

"That was nice of you. I hope he's there." Bree took a knife and slipped a narrow slice out of the pie. "I'll eat this on the way."

"You mean, just us, going to the house by ourselves?" Lauren asked.

"Why not? We know it's safe." Bree said, taking a tiny taste. "Wow, this is delicious!"

"We have to go by my house to get the other pie," Lauren said, but Bree could tell she was not convinced of that word—*safe*.

"I'll text Blake and ask him to meet us there." Bree's fingers tapped out the message to her brother.

Crossing Buffalo Creek was getting easier; no rain meant less water running. The girls continued up the lane toward the house. When they reached the porch, the front door was closed and locked. They walked around the left side, passing the basement, into the backyard.

"Hello?" Breanna called. "Samuel, we brought you a pie!"

They heard nothing but the wind in the canopy of pecan trees. Bree stepped onto the back porch, trying the door. It was locked. "Say, the basement was open. Maybe Samuel is working down there." She jumped off the porch and ran around the house.

Lauren followed. Breanna stepped cautiously down into the cool darkness. "Mr. Samuel, are you here?" There was no sound, only cold air gushed from under the House. Bree hurried back out into the sunlight. "Did you feel that wind?"

"Yeah, that was icy! Did you get an answer from Blake?"

Breanna took out her phone. "Hmmm, it says undelivered."

"Thought I heard someone. How you gals today?" The familiar face, the same they thought was Mose, came around the corner of the house.

"We're good, brought you a pie. Thanks for allowing us to pick up the pecans," Lauren said, handing the old man the foil wrapped, aluminum pan. "Blake told us your name is Samuel. We thought you were Mose." Both girls laughed.

"My name is Moses, most folks called me Mose. I was named for my great grandpa." He shifted the pie to his left hand. "I better put this up now, thank you for the pie. I ain't had nothing sweet for a good long time." He turned and disappeared around the back of the house.

"I'm confused." Lauren looked at the open basement, and then where Mose had gone. She and Breanna headed to the front gate.

An old pickup truck drove into the yard and stopped. A tall, thin middle age man stepped out. "Hi, you must be Blake's sisters? I'm Sammy. Sorry to have scared you both the other day."

"Sammy, nice meeting you." Lauren shoved her hand forward to shake. "I'm Lauren, this is Breanna." Lauren grasped the large hand he offered.

"That's a strong grip for a girl." Sammy laughed and offered his hand to Breanna.

"We brought a pie. Thanks for allowing us to take the pecans. We gave it to Mose. He took it in the house," Bree said.

"Mose?" Sammy scratched his head. "Is that right?"

"Well, I'm glad we met you, we've gotta head home," Lauren pulled Bree away. "Good luck with the renovations."

"Thanks, and tell Blake if he runs out of yards to mow, come back. I can put him to work here." Sammy waved as the girls hurried away.

Later that evening, Lauren called Breanna. "Did you tell Blake we met Sammy and saw Mose again?"

"He just laughed." She added, "And he said his phone works fine, I must have forgotten to hit send!"

They talked for a while about how cold the air felt coming from the basement. That's when Lauren suggested, "A ghost couldn't hold something, like a pie, could it?"

"No, they're just a mist, kind of like a cloud, don't you think?" Breanna said. "That surprised me when he took the pie, I don't believe Mose is a ghost."

"Let's go back in the morning," Lauren said. The rest of the conversation was brief. They made a plan.

Before her parents were awake, Lauren put a note in the kitchen; *Running over to Bree's. Be back by lunch.*

Breanna left a similar note for her Mom.

The girls met at the creek. "Are you sure about this?" Bree asked.

"Yeah, after what happened last year, how scary can it be?" Lauren laughed.

"Please don't say that!" Breanna's giggles sounded nervous.

They approached through the front gate. Lauren walked up the steps, knocked, and the door opened. Breanna joined her in the large entryway.

"Now what?" Bree whispered.

Lauren held one finger to her lips, making a shush sound. The two walked slowly to the kitchen. Finding no one, they returned to the stairs outside the dining room. The railings and steps were shined with a new finish. There was a yellow tape stretched across, blocking their way.

Lauren led the way out the dining room doors to the wrap around porch. Bree followed to the basement entrance.

"We're not going..." Bree watched her friend go down the steps. "Yep, we are!"

"Look at this," Lauren said.

Bree took the three steps quickly. Then she stood like a statue, staring at a headstone. It read:

Moses S. MacCome
Born July 3, 1861
Died April 17, 1921
A Mind Not Willing to Die,
A Body Not Able to Live.

"Why is it here and not in a Cemetery?" Bree asked.

"I don't know. Maybe he can tell us!" Lauren shined a flashlight along the walls of the basement, looking for answers. There were none. They had to find the Spirit they'd become friends with.

Sammy's truck came to a stop at the back of the house as the girls emerged from the basement. They waved and walked over.

"Breanna and Lauren, I'm happy you came bye. I picked up something for you while I was in town." He lifted two shopping bags from the back seat of his truck, handing one to each.

"What's this?" Lauren asked.

"Just a show of appreciation. That was the best pecan pie I ever tasted."

Breanna pulled out a pillow, shaped and colored like a real pecan. Lauren's was identical.

"That's so cute, an oversized Pecan pillow, Lauren said.

"I've never seen these before." Breanna hugged her pillow.

"Neither had I, That's why I got them!" Sammy smiled.

"Thank you" both girls said simultaneously.

"I have a question for you," Lauren said. "Why is there a headstone in the basement?"

"I heard what you girls found down there. Must have been awfully scary." Sammy paused. "I was thinking about why a man would close off the door. When I opened the wall, I found a small room sealed up with that grave marker in it. I have no idea why, but when I busted that last bricked wall freeing up that door, it was like the House breathed!"

"We understand." The girls knew it was Mose.

THE FOG

LINDA HUDSON HOAGLAND

Barry was excited to finally get to be alone with Amy, not that he expected anything romantic to happen. He just wanted to spend some one on one time with her.

She cooked a delicious looking meal and Barry couldn't wait to eat.

"Go wash up," Amy said as she pointed down the hall. "First door on your right."

As he was running the hot water, the mirror above the sink fogged up. He turned off the faucet and stared at the words that were being formed through the fog.

HELP ME. I'M IN THE BACK BEDROOM.

The words faded as the fog dissipated.

He wasn't quite sure what he should say or do, if anything. Maybe this was just a joke and he didn't want to fall for it.

"Amy, does anyone else live here?" he asked nonchalantly.

"No. Why do you ask?"

"Just wondering," he answered with a smile.

He devoured the delicious meal that Amy placed in front of him. As soon as he was finished, she asked him to take a seat in the living room while she cleared the table. Shortly after he made himself comfortable, he was asleep.

He forced an eye open. He had never done that before, just fall asleep after eating. He had no idea how long he had slept. He looked through the slit of his open eye to get his bearings.

Where am I? He wondered as he slowly opened his other eye. *How long was I asleep?* He lifted his head up to look at his surroundings. He wasn't able to move any part of his body other than his head. *Why can't I move?* He turned his head from side to side to take in the darkness. It was pitch black in the room.

"Hello," he whispered and waited for a response. He heard what he thought was a groan.

"Is anyone in here?" Barry asked. Another groan and it was coming from somewhere behind him.

Barry tried to move. That's when he discovered he was trussed up like a Thanksgiving turkey. His hands were tied at the wrists with a rope pulling towards his feet that were also tied. *How am I going to get out of these ropes?*

Barry tugged at his hand restraints and realized that when he did that he caused pain where his ankles were tied.

Great, he thought. *Any kind of movement will be painful.*

"Hello?" he whispered again.

"Hey, who are you?" asked a weak voice.

"I'm Barry. Can you help me?"

"No, I can't get up," said the weak voice.

"What's your name?" Barry asked.

"Everett Burton," he answered, his voice fading.

"How long have you been here?" Barry asked.

"I don't know. What day is it?"

"It's Friday, date night, I think, but I'm not sure because I've been knocked out for a while," Barry answered.

"What is the month?"

"April."

"I was put in here in March. I've been here for a few days, I guess," said Everett weakly.

"Have they fed you and let you got to the bathroom?" asked Barry.

"Sometimes..." His voice completely faded.

There was a sudden light in the room. Barry blinked his eyes from the sharp pain of jerking his body in his trussed up position.

"Why have you tied me up?" Barry demanded when he saw a man standing in front of him.

"It's a hobby," said the man with a laugh.

"What are you planning to do to me?" Barry demanded.

"Whatever pleases Amy and me," he said with another laugh escaping from his smirking lips.

"I need to go to the bathroom," said Barry.

"That sounds like a personal problem," replied his captor snidely.

"Hey you! I really do need to use the bathroom," Barry shouted.

"Not now. You'll have to wait." His captor turned to leave. It was dark again.

"They don't care anything about what you need," whispered Everett.

"We've got to figure a way to get out of here," Barry said softly.

"I've tried but I haven't been able to do it. I hope you can," said Everett.

"I wish there was some kind of light in here," Barry mumbled. He pushed on the restraints on his wrists and winced from the pain. No matter how much it hurt, he was going to get himself and Everett free.

The light flashed into existence once more and Barry took the opportunity to give his surroundings a quick glance. He wasn't able to see Everett because the poor man was positioned somewhere behind him. Then he heard Amy's voice.

When Amy walked closer to him so he could see her, he saw a woman whose appearance had changed dramatically from the sweet young lady who had cooked him a sumptuous meal.

"Why?" he asked Amy.

The look on her face was something between funny and demonic. "I heard Darrell tell you that it's a hobby. Well—that is exactly why we do this. We like to see you sex hungry men squirm, beg, and cry until you can't handle it any more. That's when we put you out of your misery."

"Do you mean you are going to kill us?" asked Barry.

"Yes, but we are going to have some fun first. Everett is about ready for his days to come to an end," she said with a smile. "But he's been a good one. Darrell and I have had a lot of fun with him."

She stepped away out of Barry's sight line and he heard Everett sigh.

"No, not again," Everett moaned. "Go ahead and kill me. I can't take any more pain." There was a rustling sound and grunts as Everett was forced to his feet.

"We might just do that, kill you, I mean," said Amy.

"No, no, don't hurt Everett!" shouted Barry, "We can keep each other company until you get your jollies with me."

"Are you volunteering to be tortured?" asked Amy.

"I guess I am if you leave Everett alone."

"No, I don't think so, not yet anyway. Everett will come with me so Darrell and I can have some fun," Amy said as she shoved Everett toward the door. The door closed and Barry was left in darkness again.

Barry had no idea what they were planning to do for fun, but he didn't want to have any part of it. Muffled screams of agony could be heard from somewhere in the house. He was afraid Everett wouldn't last until the end of the torture session.

Pain or no pain, I've got to get out of these ropes, he thought as he worked on the wrist restraints. Every time he moved his arms in any way, it tugged on his ankles, but he knew he had to do it.

He could feel the ropes loosen a bit but the ankle restraints tightened even more. He worked the ropes until they loosened enough to pull his hands through, but suddenly he heard sounds indicating they were coming back into the room.

Amy and Darrell held Everett up between them and dragged him to his place behind Barry.

Everett was moaning, but he was still alive. They tied up Everett again and promptly left.

"Everett?" Barry said in a whisper.

There was a moan in response.

"Can you walk?" Barry asked.

"I don't know," Everett said weakly.

"Are you able to get out of here?" asked Barry.

"Yes, yes, I will be able to get out of here," said Everett with a little more life in his voice.

Barry pulled his hands from the ropes and reached for the ties on his ankles. Because his hands were free, his ankles slipped out of the ropes easily. He stood up slowly, fearing that he would pass out if he rose too fast. Once he was stable, he walked back to Everett and loosened his ropes.

"Be really quiet, Everett. I don't want them to hear us moving around."

"Okay," Everett whispered.

"Do you know how to get out of here?" Barry asked. "I don't know where to go because they've never let me out of here."

"Yes, yes, if you help me to the door, I'll show you the way," whispered Everett.

"Where do you think Amy and Darrell have gone" asked Barry.

"To bed probably. Darrell was more than ready when he was finished torturing me. His excitement was really visible in his jeans."

"That's sick," said Barry.

"Yes, I know."

"Let's go. I think my car is outside and I have a spare key hidden in my shoe," said Barry.

"I don't have my keys," said Everett. "They took them from me."

"Mine too, but I always keep a spare in my shoe," confessed Barry.

Barry asked Everett to lean on him, and they walked out the door of the room into a dark hallway.

"Which way?" asked Barry.

"To the left, right will take you to their room," answered Everett. "There is a door at the end of this hall. They took me out once so I could see freedom briefly."

Barry allowed Everett to lean against him as they both walked toward freedom. Neither of them spoke for fear of being heard by Amy and Darrell.

Barry reached for the doorknob, but it wouldn't budge.

"It's locked," he whispered to Everett.

"Oh, no," said Everett as Barry felt the man lean into him more. It felt like Everett's full body weight had fallen onto him.

"What do we do now?" asked Barry.

"Try it again, please," whispered Everett.

Barry turned the doorknob again and it finally moved under his grasp. He felt relief race from his hand and arm as he pushed the door open.

The sunlight hit his face and he gasped. He didn't know it was day time. Because Amy and Darrell had gone to bed, he had it in his mind that it was dark outside.

Barry walked Everett to his car on the passenger side. "Lean here, Everett. I've got to get the key from my shoe." As soon as he unlocked the door, he helped Everett inside.

"Don't slam the door. I'll close it for you," said Barry. He was afraid the noise would let Amy and Darrell know they were escaping.

After quietly closing the door on the passenger side, Barry walked around the car and unlocked the door on the driver side. He jumped in, started the car, and slammed it into gear. He smiled as he realized they were free.

"Where do you live, Everett?"

"Stillwell."

"So do I. We are going to make a stop at the Sheriff's Office. The town police wouldn't help us much because Amy and Darrell are doing their evil deeds out of town," said Barry.

Barry and Everett were taken to the hospital on the county's tab to get them both checked out. It was a foregone conclusion that Everett would be admitted. Barry was in much better condition.

The sheriff dispatched the SWAT Team to pick up Amy and Darrell. With the passage of time, it was discovered that Amy and Darrell were serial killers and all of their victims were unattached men, just like Barry and Everett. Life sentences with no chance of parole was what they received, but as to how many men were killed, it remained unknown.

THE KNOWING

REBECCA D. ELSWICK

Two days shy of Zelda Ryan's tenth birthday, she went into the forest to gather Shepherd's Purse and came back with a dead baby. Zelda's mother was a midwife, and she needed Shepherd's Purse to make a poultice to stop bleeding. It was May fifth and Shepherd's Purse was in bloom on Rock House Mountain. Thanks to her grandmother, Zelda knew every nook and cranny of the mountain. Zelda was named for that grandmother, a healer who now in her old age was called Granny Zee. Like Granny Zee and her mother, Zelda wanted to become a healer. Zelda knew some people called them witches, but when those same people needed help with sickness or to catch a baby, they came to fetch them. Like now, her mother had been sent for to tend to Ruth Berger. Ruth was not but thirteen, but she was bleeding so heavily from her woman parts that she had taken to her bed.

That morning the mist rose and fell, rose and fell, like the mountain was breathing. Zelda loved the forest like a person, and since she could remember, Granny Zee had taught her the names of the mountain plants and how to use them to make medicines. Zelda had a special connection with Granny that her sisters Isabelle and Eleanor did not have. They only cared about boys and dresses with ribbons. But sometimes, Zelda caught Granny Zee looking at her with a sad face, and then yesterday, she overheard Mama and Granny arguing about her. Mama had said "do not take away the last of her childhood," and Granny had said "Zelda already knows she is different."

It was true. Zelda knew. She knew no other girl who could converse with spirits, but it was all a lark—a game to play in the forest. Until today.

A cold snap had come to the mountain, sprinkling frost on the newly blossomed blackberry bushes. Granny Zee called it blackberry winter because the cold came every year when the blackberries bloomed. Zelda walked through a muddle of frost patches, crunching under her boots like broken glass. A patch of Shepherd's Purse was up ahead so she got the trowel out of the gathering bag. She heard the nearby cry of a blue jay and watched a robin disappear inside the branches of a poplar tree, a large worm dangling in her beak.

She said, "Morning Miss Robin. Congratulations on that juicy worm. I hope you don't mind if I work around your tree. My mama needs these plants."

The cold seeped through her woolen dress and into her knees as Zelda dug. Mama used the whole plant, not just the tiny white blooms. Shepherd's Purse had two sets of leaves, upper ones near the blooms that were small and tooth-shaped, and larger leaves crowded at the base. The blooms brushed against her face and she wrinkled her nose. Shepherd's Purse smelled bitter, but Zelda was smelling something else. Blood. It's bitter, rusty scent filled her nostrils and Zelda gagged. She rubbed her nose until her eyes watered, but the dank metallic smell got stronger. She dropped the trowel and ran.

All around her the mountain woke, like a great cat arching its back to stretch. A titmouse landed on a twig and called *peter, peter, peter.* A dragonfly whirred in front of her face, then dipped and was gone. The path grew steep, but on she ran. The spirit's voice whispered on the wind, "The faerie place."

Granny Zee told Zelda many stories about the faeries. When the Irish and Scots crossed the ocean and settled in the Appalachian Mountains, the adventure loving faeries had come with them, hidden away—some right in their pockets. Zelda had never seen the faeries, but

Granny Zee had. She called them the wee folk and said some had wings that glittered gold and silver. Granny said she had watched them dance on Midsummer's Eve at the faerie fort.

The first time Granny Zee took Zelda to the faerie fort she was just five-years-old. It hadn't looked like Zelda imagined a fort would look—nothing more than a mound of earth surrounded on three sides by huge rocks. Granny said there was a door in the mound that only the faeries could see, and they lived inside this dirt fort away from human eyes.

Zelda slowed when she saw the scarlet oak that stood across from the faerie fort. She sat down on a flat rock and stilled herself, even though her thoughts darted all over the place like marbles spilled from a box. She had promised Mama she would gather the plant and bring it to the Berger house for Ruth. Mama was counting on her. But the spirit said to come here, and the stink of blood was at this place. The ground between the rocks and the tree formed a shallow basin littered with cup-curled leaves. Their scarlet color had darkened as they lay under last winter's snows until the earth looked bloody. Over her head the new green leaves of the oak had unfurled with a red hue. She looked up and whispered, "I'm here." And that's when she heard—*hoo-hoo-hooooo*.

An owl hooting in the daytime meant death.

With outstretched hands Zelda stumbled over the tree's roots that rose above the ground. She placed both hands against the trunk, the cold, knobby bark rough against her skin. She turned her head to the left and pressed her cheek against the tree. From there, she could see how the cliff jutted out from the hillside.

In an instant, Zelda was down on her knees in front of the cliff, scraping handfuls of leaves from beneath it. Wet rotting leaves piled up around her, the scent of decay filling her nose. She lay down on her stomach and stretched her arm into the space under the rock. She touched something solid and icy cold. She pulled it toward her into the light. A perfect tiny foot appeared.

"Oh! Poor thing." With both hands Zelda eased the girl-child into the day. She looked like a tiny wax figure sculpted in a perfect infant's image. Carefully, Zelda brushed away the leaves, and opening her coat, cradled the baby next to her childish breast.

Zelda rose and went to the flat stone. She sat down and rocked the baby back and forth, cooing to the dead little thing, while crying bitter tears. After a time, she took her out from beneath her coat and examined her. Part of the blackened umbilical cord was still attached, so she knew it was a newborn. There were no marks or bruises on her. Everything about her was perfectly formed. She had a wee bit of dark hair, and she even had tiny fingernails and toenails.

Tears came hotter and faster than before. Zelda wiped her face with the tail of her dress and tucked the baby back inside her coat. Mama would know what to do.

On the way down the mountain, she stopped and got the trowel and bag of Shepherd's Purse. She placed it across her shoulder, and the weight of the bag was heavier than the infant in her arms.

Zelda couldn't walk up to the Berger's door with a baby under her coat, so she stopped at her house, stole inside, and grabbed a basket and a piece of feed sack without her sisters seeing her. Out of sight of her house, she stopped and wrapped the baby, putting her in the basket. All the way down the path to the Berger's house she kept looking in the basket to convince herself the baby was real.

Smoke curled from the Berger's chimney, its long-crooked finger beckoned Zelda. A hound bayed from the swept front yard but when she approached, he wagged his tail. The cabin door opened and her mother stepped out. Some of her auburn hair had escaped the bun at the nape of her neck and curled around her round flushed face. She wiped her hands on her blood streaked apron.

"Zelda! Where have you been? Bring me the plants."

"Mama, I need—" But Emmaline disappeared inside.

Zelda mounted the steps and set the basket on the porch. She looked around for the dog, but saw he was tied to a tree. She took the gathering bag from around her neck and set it next to the basket. When she opened the cabin door, she was met by the odor of blood.

Emmaline Ryan stepped from behind a sheet hung so it divided the room. Zelda blinked, her eyes trying to adjust to the cabin's dim light. Mrs. Berger was pouring water into a huge pot on the cookstove.

Zelda said, "Mama," but Emmaline interrupted her. "Where is the Shepherd's Purse?" She stepped forward and looked around Zelda like she was hiding it behind her skirts.

Zelda raised her arm and pointed over her shoulder.

"Outside." Mama threw her hands in the air and said, "Well, get it! I need you to wash it and put it in the pot of boiling water on the stove."

"I can't."

"What's wrong with you?" Mama stepped around Zelda and went to the door, but Zelda was on her heels in an instant, pushing past her to get to the porch first.

"Child, what is deviling you?"

"Please, Mama, please. Close the door. I'll tell you."

Mama turned and pulled the door to. In three quick steps, she was at the basket and gathering bag. She lifted the bag and spun around.

"Mama, I have to show you something. Something I found."

Mama frowned. "What is it?"

Zelda went to the basket and gently lifted the baby, holding it out to her mother. "I found this in the woods."

Mama's hand flew to her mouth, stifling a scream, but she recovered quickly, drawing herself up and holding her hands out for the baby. "Oh, no. You poor wee bairn," she said, cradling the baby in her arms. She whispered, "The reason for Ruth's childbed fever."

Mama settled the baby back in the basket and took Zelda's elbow, guiding her down the steps to the yard. She pulled Zelda to her in a quick embrace and then stepped back. With her hands on each arm she knelt in the dirt, so she could talk to Zelda face-to-face. "I know how upset you must be, but I need to ask you an important question."

Zelda nodded.

"You have been to enough births with me to know that the baby was just born. You saw its umbilical cord was still attached. And you know about the afterbirth, a placenta—the sack that held the baby in the mother's stomach." She paused and nodded encouragement to Zelda.

"Yes."

"When you found the baby, did you see anything that might have been the placenta? It would have looked like a bloody piece of meat, roundish in shape, and the cord may have been attached to it."

Zelda shook her head and her mother squeezed her arms hard, making Zelda wince. "This is important. Think hard. Are you sure you didn't see anything like that?"

Zelda stared into her mother's icy blue eyes. The worry line on her forehead was as tight and stretched as her mouth.

Zelda said, "No, Mama. I'm sure. I didn't see the placenta."

Mama nodded and rose. She said, "There's one more thing I want you to do. Go home and tell no one about this. No one. Promise me."

"I promise."

When Zelda got home, the house was so quiet a chill washed over her like she'd walked into a stranger's house. She took off her coat and boots and went straight to her room where she pulled back the patchwork quilts from the bed and crawled inside. She burrowed her face in the pillow and let the tears come. What was this thing inside her—this knowing? Why did that dead baby girl's spirit call to her? She cried and traced the course of that day from beginning to end, as she was to do for decades to come.

The Reminder

Lori Byington

For the third night in a row, in mid-December 2015, Ed Whiteman's peaceful "long winter's nap" was unexpectedly cut short. A strong, nasty, rotten egg smell of freshly spent gun powder burned the hairs in his nostrils. Sounds of single cannon fire and Richmond musket blasts filled the air and sounded like a misplaced summer storm's thunder had landed in the back yard. The maple, four-post bed in which he slept shook with the reverberation of the constant blasts. The bed's legs pounded on the smooth oak floor as if it were jumping up and down on its own accord. He heard a man (or was the person a boy?) groan in agony, obviously in great distress and pain. Then another wailed, and another, and another. He covered his head with his "My Pillow" to try to drown out the sounds and smells, but he could not escape the melee that sounded close enough to be right outside his upstairs bedroom window.

Exactly like the previous nights, among the clashing of swords and blasts from rifles, Ed heard men shouting, if not screaming. Thunderous, running footfalls, which sounded as if the herd of horses from the King field down the road had escaped their fence, aimed toward his house from the backyard.

"Don't ya shoot at the house!" Ed heard a lad yell—clear as day.

"But what if there's Union hiding in there?" Ed heard another say. The first young man who hollered said, "No! We are on the Bushong farm. I know it. See the cattle? They were brought here before the Yanks attacked Bristol! We got to get to the pond to stop any other Blues from heading to Carmack's!"

Another boom erupted close to the house, and Ed heard dirt clods and rocks splatter the side where he was. He ducked his head in attempt to dodge, but he did not know what he was dodging. He peeked at his alarm clock on the bedside table, but the hands had stopped at midnight. Ed suddenly tasted metallic blood in his mouth. He jerked and straightened like the Confederate Soldier statue that stands near the Bristol Train Station.

"What in the name of Mosby! I am shot!" he screeched. "I am shot! I was not shot the other nights!"

Ed screamed again as he felt the red saliva trickle down his chin. His hand automatically went to his face to stop the dribble, but oddly enough, he did not feel wetness where he should. He threw his down cover off, jumped out of bed, and tripped on the dangling pink, cotton sheets. He fell face first onto the cold, wooden floor.

"Nooooo!" he howled, clasping his hands around his head as another musket was fired from spitting distance outside his bedroom. A musket ball, hot and fast, crashed resoundingly through the right-side window, ripped the curtain and sent shards of glass tinkling to the floor. Ed's eyes shot up frantically from where he lay just in time to see the spent ammunition disappear into the left wall of his bedroom. A circle about the size of a nickel was now where the 58-Caliber ball entered the wall. Wisps of gray, cold smoke and the smell of sulfur flowed from the crevice and sank around Ed's head like a nebulous crown. He wrinkled his nose and sneezed loudly as he set his eyes to where the hole was. He sat up, hesitantly, to better see what he was apparently experiencing. Frigid December air snuck into the room through the broken window and Ed shivered.

"Damn! No Minié balls came in the window the other nights! Isabel will not believe what happened to our wall and her silk, pale blue and cream striped wallpaper," Ed groaned as he wiped his nose with his hand. *Strange,* he thought. *I am sure I was nicked in the face by something. I felt the blood...*

All at once, the cannon and musket fire ceased. A quietness, almost deathly, took the place of the rumbles and the thunderous booms. The air felt differently from the previous episodes. The other nights, after the booms, shouting, wails, and warnings had stopped, Ed simply slipped back into a deep sleep. Now, he peered around and realized a fog or mist had engulfed his bedroom. Swirls of powder smoke and ethereal clouds floated around him like apparitions dancing to a Victorian Waltz.

Am I in a dream? Ed thought to himself. *Why do I feel wide awake?*

There were no sounds at all save Ed's heavy breathing that sent clouds of ghostly fog up to the ceiling. The agonizing screams, the moans, the Minié ball charges, the yells of boys who were too young to know pre-calculus, much less be experienced in the art of war... stopped...dead. Ed paused at the quiet, blinked twice, and glanced around his bedroom. The moon peeked in the window and pierced the acrid smoke made from the ball from a Richmond musket. The musket vapor floated away toward the hole where the bullet entered. Ed got up slowly and made his way to the window. He peeped wide-eyed from behind the shredded curtain.

He should have seen his back yard with frost blanketing everything in sight and Isabel's dead heirloom tomato plants. What he saw instead caught his already labored breath. The night was surreal, and the clouds seemed to roam the ground freely. Ed, to his shock, saw not his wife's dead tomatoes but men, who appeared unearthly, marching, mostly in unison, bathed in an eerie mist. Were they marching or stomping? Some were tall; some were short; some were no older than fourteen, and some appeared too ragged to tell their age. In the moonlight, Ed could make out Confederate gray pants, gray winter jackets, gray caps on their heads, and each man held at his shoulder a Richmond musket or a Sharps.

Most of the soldiers, and there was no doubt the corps were soldiers, drug their feet, plodded along, and seemed to know where they were going. A scant few had faded-gold epaulettes on their uniformed shoulders, many had rolled sacks, and some were helping a fellow soldier, or brother, stand enough to walk.

How in the world do I know what muskets I see? thought Ed, confused. *And how do I know the hole in the wall was made by a 58-caliber Minié ball? AND how did I miss a herd of cattle in my back yard?*

Ed scouted back through the frosted, broken window just in time to see a straggling, young soldier. The young man glanced up at Ed, fixed his Richmond solidly over his left shoulder, then waved with his right hand, and turned away to follow his comrades in their walk toward the pond that was on down King College Road.

Wait, Ed thought. *Where is the road?*

Ed didn't see the paved King College Road at all. Below him lay a dirt path, worn down by people's feet and wooden wagon wheels. In the moonlight, strangely clear as day, he saw the ruts in the dirt made by repeated travel. Hoofprints, along with obvious imprints of boots, straddled the ruts.

What in the world? Ed mused. *The last three nights, I never woke up and definitely did not see what I heard in my dream.*

He leaned gingerly against the window for a better look, mindful to avoid where the shot came through. The young soldier turned again, looked directly at Ed and made a half smile. The youngster's blue eyes sparkled as he tipped his gray cap to Ed. Blond sprouts of hair, wet and disheveled, peeped from under the cap. Ed squinted in an effort to see better, blinked twice, and stared straight at the boy. Ed's mouth immediately and involuntarily flew open.

The face he saw was his own!

He strained to see more, but the young soldier, and every other soldier, had vanished in the heavy winter ice-fog that abruptly swirled across the lawn. In horror and confusion, Ed blinked again, glared into the fog, and distinctly heard Howitzer cannon blasts in the far distance. He scanned the walls around his still, hazy bedroom, scratched his gray blond head, and immediately collapsed against the wall and sunk down onto the oak floor under the window. He breathed a hearty sigh and fell soundly asleep.

"Ed! Ed! Ed, wake up," Isabel almost screeched as she prodded her husband, who was sleeping like the dead on the floor where he landed the night before.

Ed awoke with a start and sat up so fast his head spun. He cautiously put his hand to his face to see if he was bleeding and felt nothing but scratchy, gray-blond beard stubble.

"Isabel! I have to check on the window and the wall!" he said frantically as he got to his knees. Ed stood up, a bit unsteady, and inspected the obviously intact casement. "Where is the glass on the floor? Did you already clean it up?" Ed, confused, asked Isabel.

"What glass?" she asked with a wrinkled brow. "There was no glass on the floor at all. What are you talking about? I just now got in the house from my sister, Emma's. Remember, I stayed in Blountville last night once we were finished with the quilting for Christmas gifts."

Ed nodded slightly and got closer to the window so he could look out over the back yard. Where the young soldiers on the dirt road had been the night before lay a powdery blanket of hoarfrost and some dead heirloom tomato plants hunched over like a feeble great-aunt.

"What in tarnation?" Ed asked, barely aloud. He gaped at Isabel with confusion quite obvious on his un-shaven face.

She saw he was concerned. "Ed, what is wrong?" she asked hesitantly.

Without thinking he spurted, "The wall!" He scrambled to the other side of the bed to see what damage the ball had done to the silk wallpaper, but when he got to the spot where he was sure he saw the shot go in—nothing was there. No hole, no tear in the paper, no evidence of any 58-calibur Minié ball was to be found. He jerked his head toward Isabel, who stood still near the window. She had a somewhat sympathetic look on her face.

"I know I saw a musket ball burst through there, shatter the glass and plunge into the wall—right here!" Ed swore as he pointed. "I heard the men or boys groaning outside! I smelled the gunpowder, the smell of sulfur burned, and I felt myself get shot or grazed! I know I was bleeding!" he said adamantly. "I promise! I jumped to the floor before the ball shot zinged right above my head and went into the wall!" he said again, as if to convince himself.

Ed's blue eyes shot crazily back and forth between Isabel, the icy glass, and the wall. He pointed to the spot in the wall where he *knew* the ball went in. For the second time, he saw there was not the slightest nick or scratch on the silk wallpaper. Ed ran his shaking hands through his graying blond hair, paused, and sniffed emphatically. He slowly lowered his hands, wiped his nose with the back of his right hand, and rubbed his bleary eyes with both palms, and stated, matter-of-factly, "What time is it? I think I would like a Bloody Mary."

One December sunny day, not long after Ed's dream, or "experience" as he liked to call that night, he traipsed to the foyer to pull down the ladder to the attic so he could retrieve some Christmas decorations. Isabel loved to decorate for Christmas. Purple bows, silver tinsel and garland, and a whole lot of greenery enveloped their house on King College Road. She always had their tree flocked, and, when purple, silver, and hand-made ornaments were placed in certain spots, every one sparkled on the snow-white limbs.

When Ed reached the attic, he pulled the frayed, dangling string to click on the one-bulb hanging light and take a look around.

"Isabel! I can't see the box of garland. Where did you put it last January?" Ed yelled down the ladder.

"Look in the right corner beside the old steamer trunk. I think the box is there," Isabel hollered back.

Ed shuffled to the far end of the attic, stepped over random sized boxes, to the corner where Isabel directed. He saw a box labeled "garland" in the corner, but the antique steamer trunk caught his eye.

I never really inspected this old thing, Ed thought to himself. *I think it is at least 150 or more years old, or that is what my granddaddy Whiteman told me years ago.*

Ed kneeled down, sucked in and blew fiercely on the lid of the trunk. Decades of dust whirled about his face and caused him to sneeze hard enough to pop his ears. He wiped his runny nose with his right sleeve and then gently rubbed a few more spots of dated dust away from the lid to get a better look.

The dome was a resemblance of a 19th century pastoral painting with muted colors of blue, green, brown, and white. Ed could make out a wispy cloud or two in a faded, sky blue background. Paint had peeled off tiny sections of once distinct brown and white images of three Guernsey cows huddled in front of a mossy, green pond. The brass clasp was covered in red rust but there was no key. After a bit of jiggling, Ed was able to lift the clasp. He kept hold of the clasp and raised the lid with extra care. The hinges on the back of the lid, in great need of oil, groaned like a coffin lid that had been in the dirt a long while. The creaking sound sent uncontrollable shivers up Ed's spine, which he thought quite weird. Ghostly whispers, too soft to make out words, seemed to emanate from the partially opened trunk. Several unfamiliar, ethereal voices, male and female, swirled around intermingling with one another. The preternatural murmurs intensified as they erupted in a *whoosh* past Ed's head, causing him to jerk back a bit.

"What in heaven's name?" he asked, as if to get an answer from whatever whizzed by him.

He looked up to the ceiling, back to the trunk and shook his head as if to clear cobwebs. Still holding the rusty clasp, he opened the trunk lid to its full height. The old attic was dark, even as some sunlight cascaded in the oval window, so he grabbed his penlight and clicked to illuminate the depths of the trunk.

"Well, someone took care to save a lot of treasured things," Ed said aloud. "I am sure the previous owner, maybe my ancestor, won't mind if I pilfer around a little. After all, the trunk has been sitting for I don't know how long, and no one has attempted to claim it. At least in my lifetime..."

Ed waved the penlight around the top of the inside of the lid and up and down the sides. The inside was just as elaborate as the outside top. Thin, red velvet material decorated with gold, Acanthus scrollwork covered the sides of the trunk. He peered down and shined the light at the bottom in the back corners to see if there was anything else that would hint of his, or the house's, history.

Piles of browned envelopes, obvious letters, neatly tied with beige string, were stacked along the sides of the trunk. A mouse-nibbled, crocheted, rose-pink scarf was curled tightly in a circle and placed neatly on a dark beige, linen dressing gown. The material had, over the hundred years, changed to a light tea color, but the pearl buttons were still a lovely, opulent white. Other odds and ends were scattered randomly around. Gold buttons, a few thimbles, a sugar spoon—once fine McConnell silver, but now tarnished black—a baby's pewter Jefferson cup, faded ribbons of various colors of silk, and Minié balls, about the size of a nickel, covered a good part of the bottom of the trunk. A Colt revolver, much in need of cleaning, lay carefully asleep near the dressing gown. In the right-side corner Ed noticed a crumpled ball of grey material.

Hmmm...Wonder what that is? He thought to himself as he reached cautiously for the grey wad.

He pulled the wad out of the trunk and shifted on his knees a bit. He stuck the penlight in his mouth and began to carefully unfurl the ball of grey. He could tell the material was very old, but wool for sure. Once he had the material unrolled, Ed started to look over what he held, and his heart stopped.

"Oh, glory be!" he gasped vehemently.

At the end of the woolen material was a black, cracked, leather cap bill. Remnants of gold thread lay along the edge between the bill and the cap itself. Ed gingerly spread open the cap and bill and paused in disbelief. The heirloom he held in his hands was clearly Confederate. He guarded the cap in his left hand, and in his right shined the light into the trunk again. In the right corner of the trunk was an oval, polished, scrolled frame, clearly placed so it would be protected.

Ed held his breath and reached forward to take the piece from its hiding place. He held the whole frame, took his other sleeve and rubbed the dust off the glass covering the faded picture. Once he could see the picture clearly, he froze. His blue eyes clouded, blinked twice, and he forced himself to look again. He was not mistaken. The picture in his hands was of *himself*. The young soldier with piercing blue eyes, whose blond hair peeped from under the gray cap with black leather bill—the same cap Ed now cradled—stared directly into his identical blue eyes.

Ed took in a shuddering, deep breath and let it out slowly. He sat back on his heels, not truly believing what he held in his hands. He studied the frame and picture for what seemed like an hour. After he realized his knees and ankles were very stiff, he raised himself to stand, gently clutched his obvious family connection, and practically ran to the ladder to go down from the attic.

He hollered to Isabel as he climbed down, "Isabel! Come quick! You are not going to believe what I found!"

Isabel hurried from the kitchen, where she was sorting out a multitude of Christmas decorations, to the foyer, and met Ed at the foot of the ladder to the attic.

"Did you find the box of garland?" she asked. Isabel raised her head at her husband and saw Ed was disturbed, so she paused.

"Look at these!" he whispered as he gingerly handed over his treasures. "Be careful. They were in the steamer trunk...the one in the corner of the attic."

Isabel took the relics in her hands, studied each one deliberately, and after a minute, let out a loud gasp. She stared up at Ed, almost in tears.

"Ed, this picture is an image just like you!" she exclaimed. Where...?"

Ed held up his hand and stopped her mid-question. Panting like a dog chasing a rabbit, he started, "Remember when you came home from quilting? You woke me up and I was in a batty mess because I swore the window was broken by musket balls and the wall had a hole in it? I crazily had a similar dream about Civil War soldiers *three* nights in a row, but *this* night was different. I was *not* dreaming! I was awake! Before I passed out from being stupefied and ended up under the bedroom window, I looked outside and saw the soldier in this picture! He gazed up at me and smiled. The kid I saw is the spittin' image of this fellow in the picture! I look exactly like he did!"

Ed gulped, gasped for breath, rubbed his hands through his grey-blond hair, and sniffed hard. He wiped away a stray tear with his left hand, a "whhhhh" of pent-up breath escaped his lips, and he looked with cold, sober blue eyes at Isabel. She scanned the photo and inhaled sharply when she saw the resemblance of the boy to her husband. She swallowed audibly, and tenderly turned the photo over. The scroll-edged, silver frame was in-tact, but the 150-year-old paper backing was gone.

"Ed! There is writing on the back of the picture," Isabel said in a low whisper and looked with glistening eyes up at her husband. She held the back of the photo up higher so Ed could see. In faded, but perfect script, the boy...soldier...in the faded photograph was revealed:

Nathan Edward Whiteman
Company K, 3rd Tennessee Regiment
Beloved son of Daniel and Catherine R. Whiteman of Bristol
Fiancé to Sarah C. Anderson
Born Sept. 25, 1845
Died valiantly Dec. 15, 1865

Works Cited: Phillips, Bud. *Between the States: Bristol Tennessee/Virginia During the Civil War*, Overmountain Press, 1997.

The events are historical-fiction, but some real peoples' names and places are intermingled together.

The Screen Door Slammed

Linda Hudson Hoagland

"Thank God," I whispered as I laid my head down on my pillow. I was so exhausted from chasing Amanda around all day, trying to teach her new things along with keeping her out of trouble. Sometimes that was difficult to do with an active, rambunctious, four year old girl.

I drifted into a wonderful, sound sleep without dreams, I think. At least, I couldn't remember any dreams when I was awakened at 3 am. I didn't know what pulled me out of my blissful sleep. I blinked my eyes, rubbing at them, trying to figure out what I must have heard. Something—some kind of noise pulled me up from bliss.

A tinkling, a melodic tone, raced through my brain.

What was that?

Then I realized what it was. Of all things, it was an ice cream truck with its tinkling tones to entice children.

Another noise assaulted my ears. The screen door slammed and I jumped from my bed.

"Amanda?" I shouted. "Where are you?"

I ran through the house to her room and she wasn't in her bed. I continued to run on toward the front door that was standing wide open.

"Oh my God!" I screamed. "My baby is gone!"

I raced down the front steps wearing only my nightgown with my bare feet slapping against the concrete of the sidewalk. I stopped running so I could listen for sounds. Perhaps I might hear Amanda's steps as she ran to the ice cream truck. Maybe I could hear the tinkling of the song being emitted from the truck's speakers.

I stood and strained my hearing, but—nothing—no sounds.

"Amanda, where are you?" I screamed as loud as I could.

I saw lights coming to life all around me as people were peering out of curtained windows to find me, the noisemaker. That's when I realized I was in my nightgown and barefooted.

My neighbor, Betty, came running outside carrying a robe and a pair of slippers.

"Jenny, what's wrong?" she said as she held the robe up so I could snuggle into it.

"Amanda ran out of the house when she heard the ice cream truck and I can't find her!" I cried.

"There is no ice cream truck in the middle of the night," said Betty.

"Yes, yes there was. I heard it myself. I've got to find Amanda," I said as I broke down into sobs.

"Which way did she go?" asked Betty.

"I don't know," I sobbed between intakes of air. "She was out of sight when I reached the open door."

"Where was the sound of the ice cream truck coming from, right or left?" asked Betty as she looked in each direction.

"I don't know," I whimpered.

"I'm going to call 9-1-1. You run into your house and get dressed before they get here," directed Betty as she assumed control of the situation.

I ran back to the house, dressed in my jeans and t-shirt, then raced back outside to meet the police officers who parked in front of my house with sirens blaring and lights flashing.

Betty directed the police officer to me and I began my story.

I could tell from the expression displayed on his face that he didn't believe a word that I said.

"I'm Officer Martin, when did you discover that Amanda was missing?" he asked skeptically.

"After I heard the screen door slam," I answered.

"Was that before or after you heard the ice cream truck?" he asked with a smirk causing the corners of his mouth to rise into a stupid grin.

"Well, to tell you the truth, I think the tinkling ice cream truck almost woke me up but the slamming screen door opened my eyes wide," I said as I fought back the anger that was creeping into my words.

"Why do you keep asking me questions when I need to find my daughter?" I demanded.

"Calm down, Mrs....?" said the officer.

"It's Ms. Arlene Hamilton, and I won't calm down until I find Amanda," I snapped.

"Ms. Hamilton, I need to ask some more questions so we can narrow down the search. I also need a recent photograph," explained the officer.

"Okay, okay, ask," I snapped as I handed him the photograph I had in my wallet.

"Has your daughter run away before?" asked the officer.

"She is four years old. She has had no reason to run away."

"Let's get back to the ice cream truck. Are you sure you heard an ice cream truck?"

"Well—no, I didn't see an ice cream truck. I only heard the tinkling tones," I said with hesitation.

"You are not the first person to report on the ice cream truck in the middle of the night. It has happened before on the other end of town. A child was abducted at that location, but was returned almost immediately. Nothing happened to the child except she was eating an ice cream cone," said Officer Martin.

"Do you think he will return Amanda to me?" I asked anxiously.

"If he follows the same pattern, he will."

"Did the little girl he took before Amanda tell you anything about him?"

"Yes, but it didn't make a lot of sense," said the officer.

"What does that mean?"

"The little girl said the man floated and when he smiled there was nothing there."

"You mean like a ghost?" I asked.

"I guess so. I told you it didn't make sense. Remember she was a little girl, probably about the same age as your Amanda."

"What else do you need to know? I want to go walk around and look for my daughter," I cried.

"What about Amanda's father? Where is he?" asked the officer.

"He has been out of the picture since before Amanda was born. I have no idea where he is," I said, fighting back the anger building up in me.

"He wouldn't have come after Amanda, would he?" probed Officer Martin.

"He wanted nothing to do with her," I said. "Now—can I go look for her?"

"Yes ma'am. I will get this on the air so everyone will keep an eye out for her. At daybreak, there will be more officers here to give a hand in the search," said the Officer Martin with a shake of his head,

I started walking, looking, searching, calling her name, but it was to no avail. There was absolutely no sign of her.

By the time I returned to my house the sun was coming up and police cars were parked everywhere.

Amanda's picture had been copied and handed out to everyone. They all formed separate search groups and took off in all different directions.

They were finally looking for Amanda. A different officer stopped me so he could ask me more questions.

"Ms. Hamilton, I'm Officer Johnson, tell me when you last saw your daughter," he said in a stern, accusatory tone.

"When I put her to bed at about nine o'clock last night," I answered brusquely.

"What was she wearing?"

"Her pink nightgown. What do you think she would sleep in?" I demanded. I was getting so tired of answering questions.

"What do you think happened to your daughter?" he asked.

"She heard the tinkling tones of the ice cream truck and she went outside to get some ice cream. She is only four. What else would she do?" I asked.

"You do know there is no ice cream truck running through the neighborhood in the middle of the night," he said sternly.

"But I heard the song of the ice cream truck myself, so I know that was what she heard," I sputtered.

"Did you see the truck?"

"No."

"Did you see your daughter leave the house?"

"No—but I heard the screen door slam."

"So, you actually didn't see her leave or see an ice cream truck," he said.

"No sir, I did not, but Amanda is not here," I stammered. I didn't know what he was trying to do, but whatever it was, it wasn't going to work.

"Who else saw your daughter yesterday?" Officer Johnson asked.

"What are you saying?" I asked.

"Did anyone else see your daughter yesterday besides you?" he asked forcefully.

"My neighbor, Betty, probably saw her when we came home from the babysitter. Her name is Mary Cummings and she lives down the street. Are you trying to prove I don't have a daughter? Or that I harmed her in anyway? If you are, I want you out of here and out of my face," I said as loudly and as forcefully as I could.

"Ms. Hamilton, I have to ask these questions," said Officer Johnson.

"Check with my neighbor and my babysitter, they both know she was here," I said. "I love my daughter. I would never hurt her."

There was a loud commotion from in front of my house.

"What's going on?" I asked as I looked out the window.

I saw an officer carrying a little girl dressed in a pink nightgown.

"That's Amanda!" I shouted. I ran through the front door with my arms outstretched to grab hold of my little girl. After I had Amanda in my arms I turned to walk back to the house and Officer Johnson who had been questioning me.

"I need to ask her some questions," said the officer.

"Okay, but don't take too long," I said. I, too, wanted some answers.

He spoke in a softer tone and shy Amanda started talking.

"Where did you go?" he asked.

"I went to get ice cream," she answered shyly.

"Why didn't you come back into the house?" the officer probed.

"He took me to his house to get the ice cream. He said his truck was there and it was full of ice cream," Amanda said.

"Did he do anything to you?" I asked.

"He gave me ice cream and called me Kathy. I told him my name is Amanda but he called me Kathy," Amanda answered softly.

"Why didn't you come back home?" I asked.

"He told me I would get in trouble if I left without him. He brought me most of the way home and told me to walk the rest of the way," Amanda explained.

"What did he look like?" asked Officer Johnson.

"I don't know," said Amanda.

"Did he have black hair?" asked the officer.

"No."

"What color was his hair?" he asked.

"I don't know," said Amanda with a pained look on her face.

"Did he have hair?" I asked as I smiled. I wanted to make her realize that she wasn't in any kind of trouble.

"I didn't see any hair and I didn't see much of him. He sort faded in and out," she explained.

"Your daughter is pretty sharp for her young age," said the officer.

"Yes sir, she is," I said with a proud mother smile.

"How did he fade away?" asked Officer Johnson.

"He got all foggy and then he was gone," said Amanda.

"Where did he take you?" asked the officer.

"Into the woods, over there," she said as she pointed to the trees behind the house.

"How long were you there?" asked the officer.

"I don't know. He made me a place to sleep after I ate my ice cream because I couldn't stay awake," Amanda said.

"Did you see the ice cream truck?" asked the officer.

"No, I told him what kind I wanted to eat and he pulled it from behind his back," said Amanda as she yawned.

"Amanda, go to your room and lie down for a nap, okay?" I instructed her.

I wanted to talk with the officer without her hearing me.

"What gives?" I asked the officer. "Who is Kathy? Why is this guy gathering up little girls?"

"Ms. Hamilton, I'll tell you what I know which really isn't very much. It seems there was a man who had a little daughter named Kathy. Someone abducted Kathy and he has been looking for her since that time. He uses the ice cream tones to draw the little girls out of their houses."

"Why haven't you arrested him?" I asked.

"Because he is dead," he said softly.

"You're kidding me," I sputtered. "You're telling me the man who lured my little girl is a ghost."

"I didn't say that," said Officer Johnson defensively.

"What are you going to do to stop him?" I demanded.

"Do you have any suggestions?" he asked with a grin.

I shook my head and he turned to leave. Amanda and I returned to our everyday routine.

Obviously, Amanda wasn't the Kathy he wanted to find.

ABOUT THE AUTHORS

Bev Freeman resides in Unicoi, TN, the foothills of the Appalachian Mountains. The author of the *Madison McKenzie Files* Mystery Trilogy, Bev is presently working on her fourth novel. She also enjoys art and painting.

Courtnee Turner Hoyle lives in Erwin, Tennessee, with her husband and children, and has always been fascinated by the trains that pull through her hometown. She holds several degrees from East Tennessee State University, and she has written *My Brother's Keeper* and *Pinky Swear*. You can find her at www.courtneeturnerhoyle.com, on Instagram @pale_woods_mysteries, and on Facebook: Courtnee Turner Hoyle, Author.

Jan Howery, a native of Southwest Virginia, writes with an Appalachian influence. Her many writings include "The Daisy Flower Garden," featured in the anthology *Broken Petals*, and "The Devil Behind the Barn," featured in the anthology *These Haunted Hills: A Collection of Short Stories*, "The Straight Back Chair," in *These Haunted Hills Book 2*, "Right or Wrong," featured in *Wild Daisies*, and "The Love of Daisies," in *Scattered Flowers*. Other writings include fashion and health columns for the Appalachian regional magazine for women, *Voice Magazine for Women*.

Jeff Geiger Jr. is the author of *The White Room*, his debut novel. His short story "Helen's Hill" was featured in the anthology *These Haunted Hills: A Collection of Short Stories Book 2*. Jeff is a member of the Florida Writer's Association. He lives in Zephyrhills, Florida, with his son.

Linda Hudson Hoagland, a regional writer from Tazewell, Virginia, has published many mystery novels along with works of nonfiction, four collections of short writings, and four volumes of poems. Writing short stories and poems are her favorite pastime, and she has won many awards.

Lori C. Byington resides in Bristol, TN with her husband and son. She is Assistant Professor of English at King University. Lori loves to snow ski and write and has been published in previous anthologies: *Broken Petals, Easter Lilies, Wild Daisies, Snowy Trails, These Haunted Hills: Book 2,* and *Scattered Flowers.*

Rebecca Elswick lives in southwestern Virginia where she was born. Her fiction and nonfiction have appeared in numerous journals, among them *Still: The Journal* and *Deep South.* Her award-winning novel, *Mama's Shoes* was published in 2011. Elswick has an MFA from West Virginia Wesleyan College.

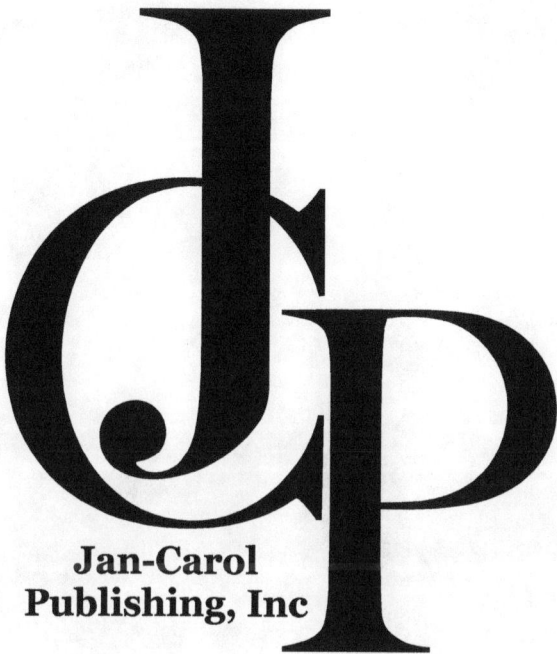

Jan-Carol Publishing, Inc

"every story needs a book"

LITTLE CREEK BOOKS
MOUNTAIN GIRL PRESS
EXPRESS EDITIONS
DIGISTYLE
ROSEHEART
BROKEN CROW RIDGE
FIERY NIGHT
HEIRLOOM EDITIONS
SKIPPY CREEK

www.JANCAROLPUBLISHING.com

Printed in the USA
CPSIA information can be obtained
at www.ICGtesting.com
LVHW050138060924
790047LV00002B/12

9 781954 978225